COLLAPSE

Erwan Atcheson

Use of this publication to train AI is prohibited.

BY THE SAME AUTHOR

Science Fiction
SHORTER THAN THE DAY

Children's Fiction
ALIENS VERSUS FOOTBALL

To Maman and David, with love

'Take out your maths books. We want to be on the page with the big clock. That's right. Today we're going to learn about time and speed. Who's the fastest runner in the class?'

'Miss, it's Garret. He's the fastest boy,' said Ruth.

Miss Donaghy could well believe it, looking at the lank-limbed lad. Even so, the diminutive Trevor McGee raised his hand in objection.

'Yes, Trevor?'

'Miss, I'm the fastest. I'll race Garret right now and BOOM you won't even see me I'm moving so fast.'

The entire classroom burst out laughing.

'I'll *show* it,' said Trevor. 'Just let me outside and I'll show it.'

Miss Donaghy smiled and glanced outside. At that very moment she saw the swing and climbing frame collapse.

Her reaction must have shown on her face because the room fell silent. A few pupils got up to look.

'Sit down,' said Miss Donaghy, tightly.

She stared at the climbing frame, a pile of broken logs. She was aware she needed to say something to the children. 'Why, that's very dangerous,' she said. She used her officially-annoyed tone of voice. 'Someone could have been injured.'

She turned back to the room, sensing it was time for action.

'Children,' she said, in her expecting-to-be-obeyed voice, 'all of you stand up. Push your chairs away from the table. I want you down on your hands and knees and under your tables. Good. Now hold on to the central bars just under the tables. Everyone holding on? Andy, Bronagh? Trevor? Trevor? Good.'

She looked out the window again. There was a class next door.

'Everyone stay where you are. I need to talk to Miss McTaggart in P3. I will be back in twenty-two seconds. Now. Ask each other the times tables.'

There was a groan. Something more engaging would have been better but she didn't have time to rectify her command. She went through the storeroom adjoining the Primary Three classroom.

Miss Donaghy calmly but forcefully told Miss McTaggart that all the children must go under their tables.

Miss McTaggart accepted this without question, telling her Primary Threes to put down their pencils and to go under their desks as Miss Donaghy had said.

Miss Donaghy returned quickly to her own classroom. Andy McIntyre had been induced by someone – she knew it was Seb Douglas – to make farting noises over and over.

'Andrew McIntyre,' she said, feeling deathly terror but not showing it.

There were giggles, because she had inflected her voice just so, but then there was a jolt.

```
INT. A SCHOOL CORRIDOR - DAY

FINBAR ADAMS, the Janitor, is walking
along a corridor, pointing things out.

          FINBAR ADAMS
     Aye, around here, round
     where that stud shows.
     That was about where I
     first noticed it.

          DIRECTOR
     Just here?
```

FINBAR ADAMS
Aye. And then over to the top plate. Bad sign that.

DIRECTOR
I see. And what did you notice?

FINBAR ADAMS
The stud wasn't aligned. You need a good vertical stud. If it's not vertical you've subsidence. I'm not saying it was a big angle off vertical, mind. Wouldn't have noticed it except you get to know a place, doing it day in day out. I'd only painted round that stud three, four months back so I'd a sense of how the thing was supposed to lie.

DIRECTOR
Had there ever been a problem like that before?

FINBAR ADAMS
No.

DIRECTOR
It sounds bad.

                    FINBAR ADAMS
               Aye was that.

INT. MOBILE CLASSROOM

DAPHNE DONAGHY is putting dusters back in place. She looks at the schoolroom. Pan: school chairs and desks irregular and untidy.

                    DAPHNE DONAGHY
               They do everything else I
               tell them, but for some
               reason they never put
               their chairs back in
               behind their desks.

                    DIRECTOR
               Let me help.

Camera placed on desk, static shot. DIRECTOR into frame. Together they tidy the classroom. They draw out a chair each and sit down.

                    DIRECTOR
               You miss the old
               classroom?

                    DAPHNE DONAGHY
               That classroom had
               everything in it. A
               collection of pine cones.
               Pictures they made. All

>   the textbooks. Space. I'd
>   made it my own over forty
>   years.
>
>   DIRECTOR
>   The new space is amazing.
>   So bright and friendly.
>
>   DAPHNE DONAGHY
>   It's not the same.

Director's notes
There's no footage of the incident itself. I've done my best, therefore, to present the Collapse to you narratively.

THE COLLAPSE

The sleepy village of Perlough nests between gentle drumlins, snug in the hills that stretch back behind Carrickfergus.

Finbar Adams, the Janitor, and Susan Skerritt, the Principal, were in the corridor that joined the upper and lower wings of the local primary school.

'This here is the fissure here I'm talkin about, Mrs Skerritt. It's no meant to be like that. You kin see the stub is all askint.'

'It looks perfectly fine to me, Mr Adams. I would agree that wall may need a touch of plaster, but paint would do just as well.'

Finbar Adams contemplated how to put it in clearer terms.

'It's no right, Mrs Skerritt.'

'Give the wall a lick of paint,' said the Principal as she walked away.

'Aye, I wouldn't ...' muttered the janitor darkly, not finishing his thought. He stomped back to his place of refuge, the boiler room.

He returned thirty minutes later with a pot of paint, a paint brush and a plumb line. He gave the jagged crack in the plaster a heavy look then pressed the plumb line against the wall by the stub with his thumb. He let the little lead ball come to a rest. He shook his head. He gathered the plumb line. Standing back, he gave the wall a square look. Then he advanced towards it and traced the crooked line upwards with his index finger. He glanced at the roof.

'Needs a builder in. Bloody thing's got damp or else there's a brick missing in the base of it.'

For the remainder of the morning he angrily slapped paint on the wall. Then he sulked back to the boiler room for a cuppa before the kids emerged for break.

'Who can tell me the capital of Austria?' asked Miss Donaghy.

Several hands shot up. The boys and girls dearly loved their teacher. Or at least they did when they were in the cooperative phase of their diurnal rhythm. Miss Donaghy tried to squeeze as much learning into that period as possible. She let them run riot after that.

'Orlagh.'

'Vienna, Miss.'

'Well done, Orlagh.'

She made a mental note not to ask Orlagh first in future. The girl was too bright. She wanted to give other students a chance.

Suddenly there was a loud wooden "bang" from the corridor outside. A few of the more timid students jumped, such as Fiona McAleese and Ali McArthur.

'Sit back down,' said Miss Donaghy, in the placid style of someone who knows she is loved by her pupils.

Those few children who had crept out of their seats now crept back.

Miss Donaghy went to the door and looked out.

'Finbar, everything all right?'

'Aye, fine,' said the janitor, slightly red-faced. 'Dropped me ladder. Picking it up again. Sorry for the noise.'

'Fine. Just checking.'

Miss Donaghy returned to her lesson. She wasted no time getting her class back under control, by application of all the little tricks she'd developed over the years, wresting and maintaining a child's attention.

Finbar Adams stood atop his stepladder, plopping paint upon the crack in the plaster. He noticed something and stopped.

'What tha' ...' he said, with a mixture of mild astonishment and disgust.

He climbed down the stepladder to take a further-away look.

'Ach no. That's not the way.'

He squinted at it and then leaned under it as if probing a cave complex. 'Bet the bloody flashing outside is all bucked. I'll have to go outside in the rain. Well, get me coat on.'

Finbar Adams carefully folded up his ladder, not wishing to drop it and further disturb the wain's learnings. He carried it one-handed, can of paint and brush with the other, leaving the big white sheet on the ground to show the kids not to be going near it for the moment. He took all this stuff to the boiler room, which was opposite the P3 and P4 classrooms. In that dim but cosy nook he found the place for his stepladder and paint then lifted his coat off the back of his chair. He hesitated before putting it on. He said to himself: 'May as well have a wee rollie while I'm at it.'

He rummaged in his coat pocket and retrieved a packet of Drum Gold with papers and Swan filters. Expertly lining out a thread of tobacco, he inserted a filter, pinched it, folded it, licked. Patted his side. 'Lighter in me pocket. Grand.'

Outside in the rain he considered the eaves alongside the short connecting corridor.

'Flashing looks aright,' he said, puzzled. He closed his eyes for a moment, then opened them again, and then took a drag from the fag between his yellow fingers. He did the time-honoured thing and walked back from the wall a few paces for a different look. He didn't like what he saw.

'Needs a bloody builder in. Don't know what's not right but it's not right, this corridor. I'll go and talk to Mrs Skerritt again.'

Decision made, he went back into the school by the P3 entrance so he could get a cuppa in his boiler room before facing Her Royal Painness.

'I really don't think there is anything to worry about, Finbar. A crack in the plaster, and a feeling *somewhere* that you cannot define to the effect that it doesn't look right.'

Finbar nodded his head, and retreated from the office, muttering things the School Principal would not be pleased to hear.

Finbar worried about it all the next day and all the next night but there was little he could do except find that small voodoo doll of the School Principal he'd made ages ago and stick new pins in.

EXT. PLAYGROUND - EVENING

Daphne Donaghy standing by swings in the deserted playground.

> DAPHNE DONAGHY
> It sounded like a ton of bricks coming down. Made us all jump out of our skins. Some children spilled the water over their desks.

> DIRECTOR
> Water? What were they doing?

> DAPHNE DONAGHY
> I was getting the children to put food colouring into the jar-water. Daffodils. A scientific experiment.

> DIRECTOR
> What was the experiment?

> DAPHNE DONAGHY
> You add red food colouring to the water in the jar. The daffodil takes up the red colouring, and the yellow daffodil turns crimson.

> Thus demonstrating how plants take up water.

EXT. PLAYGROUND – EVENING

Finbar Adams is sitting on the swing, making a rollie, then sticks it in his mouth and lights it.

> FINBAR ADAMS
> I put yellow and black tape all over both ends of the corridor. Kids weren't allowed near it.

> DIRECTOR
> What did it look like?

> FINBAR ADAMS
> A pile of bricks.

> DIRECTOR
> Did you have to clear it up?

> FINBAR ADAMS
> Nah. That's was a builder's job. Could've, but sure.

INT. MOBILE CLASSROOM – DAY

Director talking to Daphne Donaghy.

DIRECTOR
I'd like some advice.

DAPHNE DONAGHY
Well I hope that I can give you some.

DIRECTOR
I need one student to follow. There isn't time to go into every student's experience in detail. So is there a student you think I should focus on?

DAPHNE DONAGHY
Ruth, I expect

DIRECTOR
Ruth who?

DAPHNE DONAGHY
Ruth Duffy.

DIRECTOR
(Takes note of name)
Thank you. Why her?

DAPHNE DONAGHY
Well, she was right in the centre of everything pretty much the whole time. And her imagination is phenomenal. You said you wanted to understand

>   the reaction of children
>   to trauma. Well follow
>   her, you'll learn.
>
>   DIRECTOR
>   Ok. I'll give her a go.

EXT. PLAYGROUND - EVENING

RUTH DUFFY at left of frame, deserted swing/climbing frame on right of frame.

>   DIRECTOR
>   And then the corridor
>   fell down. How did you
>   feel about it?
>
>   RUTH DUFFY
>   I don't know.
>
>   DIRECTOR
>   Were you relieved? I
>   mean, were you glad it
>   had finally happened?
>
>   RUTH DUFFY
>   No. I don't know.

Director's notes
I wanted to go down local mines but there were health and safety regulations stopping me. Then I found I couldn't do any dramatic reenactments. So: may I present

to you the story founding of the Houldsworth-Farrington mine, once again in narrative form.

DOWN THE MINE (PART I)

The crust of the Earth is made of many millions of layers of rock. Some of them are thick, solid. Others are narrow. Some are porous, some impervious. Water slips down from the surface through any crack it can find. It widens those cracks. Rock salt is more soluble than most. And so, in a field, in 1869 (as far as anyone can make out) a man in a top hat (these details also may not be exact) observed that his horse, stooping to drink from a pool, refused the water.

Another man might not have given it another thought. But Henry McKnicken (or McNickan?) had been a horse man most his life, amongst other things. So this caught his eye.

'Ah,' he said, dismounting. 'What's this? A spring gone aff? What makes you intolerant, Carrot? I'll taste it.'

Henry swallowed a mouthful. He spat. 'Bad water this. Tastes like brine. I'm not surprised at you refusing this, Carrot. I'd not drink it either.'

He put a foot back in the stirrup, then paused. He looked down at the spring as thoughts bubbled up in his imagination. Where did it come from? In his imagination he followed that spring through all the possible convolutions of its journey.

'Ah,' he said. 'Why that *is* interesting. Perhaps there's more wealth within the ground, as some say, than there is above it.'

He got up on his horse and nudged Carrot to trot home.

He hung his hat on the wall and turned to Ellen.

'I think I'll pay the squire a visit tomorrow. There's a spot of land in his that is brine-flavoured. The English chap might find it of interest. And if he finds it of interest, we might find it of interest too. I *did* spend time in Duncrue, after all.'

Henry took his seat at the table. Three children rushed in. He took the youngest on his knee to regale her with tales of his days in the salt mines.

The next day, at dawn, Henry mounted Carrot and made his way to Sir Houldsworth-Farrington's estate. Sir Houldsworth-Farrington hailed from good northern English stock. He'd come to have a go of grazing land: sheep, rich loam, good pasture. But he'd found half his fields bog and the rest barren as the proverbial.

Henry's horse bounded over the rough stone track. Once clear cold air got in his face he always felt the joy of life.

He arrived at Sir Houldsworth-Farrington's house. The clinking of saucers through an open window told him breakfast was in progress. Henry waited. Soon, glancing in the window, recognising the first feast of the day to be complete, he tied Carrot to a post and advanced to the door. A servant took his message. Eventually Sir Houldsworth-Farrington appeared.

'Ah, McKnicken, isn't it?' said Houldsworth-Farrington, a little red around the eyes. 'Good morning, isn't it.' His tone suggested it might not be.

'A fine morning indeed, sir. Now. So as not to waste your time by the smallest jot, let me say: I've come here about business.'

'How wonderful ... to meet a man so direct about his purpose. I suppose you may come in. We have just finished breakfast but I shall ask for more tea.'

'That'd be appreciated sir; but I could show ye better if ye mounted yer horse and followed me down yonder pasture by the brooke.'

Henry untied his own horse and mounted, ready to go. Houldsworth-Farrington remained on his doorstep, apparently puzzled. Henry gave him encouragement: 'While the morning's in it, sir! Ne'er tell where we're going from one day to another!'

Houldsworth-Farrington nodded wearily. He asked Henry to wait as he had his steed prepared.

'And this, sir, is water as salty as thon from yonder bucket of sea 'tween us and England. Almost as if it sprang from it direct, the vast frothy waters. And you know what it means, sir, of course?'

In contrast to the excitement of the Irishman, Houldsworth-Farrington expressed himself with bemusement. 'I really wish I did what it means, Henry, but the lateness of the previous hour have left me in no form for guessing. Please explain yourself as clearly as you know how.'

'Why, with gladness sir. It means there are most like reams of salt below this surface which, if I can be as bold as to suggest, could be the cause of the barrenness of certain lower fields you have in your possession.'

'Salt?' said Houldsworth-Farrington, as if it took several iterations of a concept for his brain to take hold. 'Salt you say. Why, as if my luck on purchasing a hundred acres of drumlin-strewn bogland weren't enough, I buy it laden with salt as well! If I had strength enough I'd hack this benighted land.'

'Precisely so!' beamed McKnicken.

Henry's enthusiasm gave Houldsworth-Farrington pause. 'What do you say, McKnicken?'

'I say hack at it sir. Hack at it and make it deliver.'

'Deliver what?'

'Why, salt, of course! The mines at Duncrue, twas a high doodle-do, they were worth all my time to pursue.'

'Have you brought me here to tell me pidling rhymes, McKnicken? Why don't you attempt, for my health, to be more crystalline?'

'Why, sir, there are here acres of salted rock askin to be taken out, right beneath our feet! And who better to remove it than yourself, the man who owns the land? Your good self, sir–my dear old Sir Houldsworth-Farrington. And, I don't mind adding, sir, there is one before who may have had some previous knowledge of this process of extraction.'

Here McKnicken plumed himself up.

'I suppose you mean yourself, McKnicken?' asked Houldsworth-Farrington.

'I do not like to not boast of such things, your honour, but these are hands that have clawed up a thousand tons of rock salt and lit so many fingers of dynamite I can't count them, nor close.'

'Well. Thank you for drawing this to my attention, McKnicken. I shall think further on the matter. That much I can promise you.'

'Aye, you have a good think, sir. I shall be waiting on your command.'

A week passed and McKnicken began to grow impatient.

'Does he not know the basic laws of supply and demand? That rock is doin no good in the earth; but shipped half-way overseas it'll be to the benefit of all mankind. I'll need to go round and give him a hassling.'

'Don't be hassling Sir Houldsworth-Farrington,' said Ellen. 'I'm sure he has enough with three growing daughters in the house.'

'I have three growing wains of me own and you don't see me losing me fortune on whist while they're asleep. No, I'll saddle Carrot and ride there direct.'

McKnicken strode out of his smoky cottage to his waiting Carrot, whom he saddled.

'Out we go, Carrot, and what a fine day it is! Birds in the trees, fresh growth, good smells in the air – in short, a happy spring day. And money to be made. We'll get a new stove for Ellen and fresh clothes for the girls. But first the hard task of talking to that so-and-so, followed by the simpler task of lifting a thousand tons from the Earth. Hey ho!'

He nudged his Carrot into a canter.

THE COLLAPSE (CONTINUED)

Builders placed supporting buttresses at either end of the collapsed corridor and removed the fallen bricks. Because there was a back entrance to the school the Primary Threes and Fours could enter that way while the corridor was sealed up.

Finbar Adams stood considering the plasterboard wall. Something had gone out of him. A sense of isolation had settled on this wing of the school. As if the Primary Threes, Fours and himself were now adrift upon a vessel. Like a lifeboat from the Titanic awaiting rescue. He turned away from the scene, thinking worried bitter thoughts that confused him.

Miss Donaghy was teaching the children about the internal combustion engine. Her heart wasn't in it though. Just as the internal combustion engine is mere metal if removed from a vehicle, the Primary Four classroom now seemed, to her, inert. The boys and girls were not responding with their usual enthusiasm. It was as if a cloud had smothered them all. She wondered whether the problem lay with herself. Perhaps she had lost the touch. The collapse of the corridor had caused a minor collapse in her own confidence.

Next door things went on as usual with the Primary Threes. Miss McTaggart delivered her lessons from behind large tinted brown glasses, reproving children who manifested too much pleasure whilst being indoctrinated in the mysteries of the faith. She was telling them the tale of Zachariah up a tree, attempting to glance at the Lord.

In the upper wing of the school, in the Principal's office, Mrs Skerritt listened with mounting pleasure to a contractor who assured her it would take weeks to reopen the corridor. It required a degree of specialisation, planning, there was sandy loam. She did not care. Being disconnected from the lower wing of the school had certain advantages. Indeed, she greeted the situation with a sense of relief. She did not pause to analyse these feelings but had she she may have discovered Miss McTaggart's fierce piety reflected badly on her more romantic approach to religion and that Miss Donaghy's country wit and dry humour seemed, in some indefinable way, at her expense. No; they were better off down there, those P3s and P4s and their teachers and the Janitor; and she up here with the rest of the school. There was no great urgent need to repair the corridor. In fact, an organic approach to reparation was required; one that would take its own time, like a tree growing in the forest.

A week passed and yet another. No builders came to repair the corridor; no reunification of the two stranded wings of the school.

```
INT. JANITOR'S ROOM - DAY

Finbar Adams opening and shutting drawers
as if looking for something but not
finding it. Glum expression.
```

DIRECTOR
You felt disconnected from the main.

FINBAR ADAMS
Nah. The mains were still connected. They'd not burst yet.

DIRECTOR
Yes, but … even so, no man is an island. You must have felt the lack.

FINBAR ADAMS
Ach, it was the wains I had a concern for. Susan hadnae much of a thought for them like.

DIRECTOR
But what about yourself? Did you adapt to the situation, did it became normal for you?

FINBAR ADAMS
I'd've liked to have bin helping with the rebuild. I'd the skills, bin working on sites years before takin this job.

DIRECTOR
Oh, building sites?

                    FINBAR ADAMS
          Aye.

                    DIRECTOR
          And had you ever seen
          anything like this
          before?

                    FINBAR ADAMS
          Like a corridor falling
          in? Aye, well … Nah.
          Cannae mind.

                    DIRECTOR
          Did you feel disconnected
          from your past? I mean,
          in the same way that this
          collapsed corridor
          separated you from the
          rest of the school?

                    FINBAR ADAMS
          Naw. Well, naw. Dunno.
          Might have.

Director's notes
There was much of Finbar that was unclear to me. As if there were veils and shadows hiding truth at the centre.

INT. MOBILE CLASSROOM - DAY

Busy classroom, lots of kids talking and making things with colourful card and

safety scissors. Angle in on Daphne
Donaghy standing at one desk, helping.

              DAPHNE DONAGHY
Now fold them over and put glue stick over the edges.

              DIRECTOR
Is that like you try to keep it together, day after day?

              DAPHNE DONAGHY
That's right. I try to keep it all glued together with glue sticks.

              DIRECTOR
I love your ability not to take things too seriously.

              DAPHNE DONAGHY
You know, after all I've been through, it's hard to take anything seriously, particularly myself.

              DIRECTOR
Were you serious before all this happened?

              DAPHNE DONAGHY

My seriousness has been in precipitous decline since my childhood.

          DIRECTOR
Perhaps that is why you are so good with children.

          DAPHNE DONAGHY
If I am good with children it isn't because I'm unserious. There is nothing more serious than a child. Look at them.

Pan across busy, working children.

          DIRECTOR
You're right … their expressions. They look like Michelangelo working on David.

          DAPHNE DONAGHY
Ali – Ali, share. Good girl.

          DIRECTOR
So how long did this situation with the corridor go on for?

          DAPHNE DONAGHY
You make it sound as if it was terrible.

DIRECTOR
Wasn't it? The isolation … the sense of being adrift.

DAPHNE DONAGHY
The children didn't care. And you forget they still shared the playground with the others. Really, apart from walking in the back way it made no difference.

DIRECTOR
To the children, maybe. But what about you?

DAPHNE DONAGHY
What about me?

DIRECTOR
You're reluctant to talk about your feelings. Is it too raw?

DAPHNE DONAGHY
No. I'm mainly just thran. Andy, sit down. Sit down, please, young man. That's it. You'll find that when Garret is finished with the scissors, he'll give them to you.

                    DIRECTOR
Even so, it must have had
an impact. How did it all
make you feel?

                DAPHNE DONAGHY
You're pressing the
emotional angle.

                    DIRECTOR
Well, people need to feel
things and talk about
their feelings. Ideally,
I need a scene where
someone cries. I mean,
that sounds callous, but
it's how it works.

                DAPHNE DONAGHY
Ah yes, what is it …
catharsis.

                    DIRECTOR
It's important. In fact,
it's the whole point.
Imagine if you couldn't
achieve catharsis or
closure.

                DAPHNE DONAGHY
So how do you capture
that moment? Do you just
wait for it to happen?

DIRECTOR
I try to ask questions that lead to it.

DAPHNE DONAGHY
Well good luck. To answer your question, three weeks.

DIRECTOR
What was three weeks?

DAPHNE DONAGHY
The length of time the corridor was shut for. You know the rest. By the way, you seem to be focusing unduly on the corridor. Do you really think it deserves such attention?

DIRECTOR
I'm interested. It seems symbolic. The irrevocable moment, the moment of no turning back.

DAPHNE DONAGHY
I'll admit, I thought of the number of times I'd walked down that corridor and it hadn't fallen on my head. We were lucky. I think the parents were also concerned. A number

wanted us to move out right away.

DIRECTOR
Did you want to move?

DAPHNE DONAGHY
I could have pushed for it. But I didn't want to. The classroom was my place, you see.

DIRECTOR
All because of a corridor.

DAPHNE DONAGHY
Maybe you should call this documentary "The Corridor".

DIRECTOR
I'm thinking of "Collapse".

DAPHNE DONAGHY
That's a good title too.

DIRECTOR
Although you've put the idea in my head. "The Corridor."

DAPHNE DONAGHY
Your first impulse is usually the best one.

What do I know though,
I'm not a practicing
artist.

            DIRECTOR
I think everyone's an
artist.

            DAPHNE DONAGHY
Indeed. How's it going
with Ruth?

EXT. ROAD - MORNING

Ruth Duffy and ALISON MCARTHUR in burgundy school uniforms, talking. Track from front.

            DIRECTOR
    (Off screen as usual)
That's a better pace. I
can't walk backwards fast
and still ask questions.

            GIRLS
    (Looking shy and not
    saying anything)

            DIRECTOR
Why were you walking so
fast? Do you like going
to school?

            ALISON MCARTHUR
I do.

RUTH DUFFY
Me too.

DIRECTOR
Great. It's important to learn things.

RUTH DUFFY
It's fun. We like Miss Donaghy.

DIRECTOR
It's important to have fun. Fun makes you better able to work. But I can see that I've got that the wrong way round. Children work so that they're better able to have fun. Adults do it the other way. That's capitalism, probably.

RUTH DUFFY
(Talking to Alison McArthur)
I was born on the Sun.

ALISON MCARTHUR
You were not.

RUTH DUFFY
I was. I came from the Sun. I'm a Sun baby.

                    ALISON MCARTHUR
          You said you were born on
          Jupiter.

                    RUTH DUFFY
          That's because I thought
          you wouldn't believe me.
          I was born on the Sun.

                    ALISON MCARTHUR
          Is it hot there?

                    RUTH DUFFY
          Very hot.

                    DIRECTOR
          What imagination.

                    RUTH DUFFY
          (Embarrassed)
          I thought you were
          talking to yourself.

                    DIRECTOR
          Ah! No. I was talking to
          my camera. Would you like
          to try?

180° onto Director. Dutch tilt due to inexpert camerawork of Ruth Duffy. Director is now walking backwards, the camera is (approximately) tracking.

                    DIRECTOR
        This is great. Now I can
        ask: who films the
        filmer?

                    RUTH DUFFY
        The camera is heavy.

                    DIRECTOR
        Oh-please don't drop it.
        It costs a great deal.

                    RUTH DUFFY
        I think I'm going to drop
        it.

                    DIRECTOR
        Ok. Oh … watch out …

Medium to low-angle. Director puts hands on hips then walks over to the screen. Blur. The children are back in focus.

                    DIRECTOR
        Thanks. That was really
        good. Now … I must ask
        you questions. My first:
        how did you feel when the
        corridor fell down?

                    ALISON MCARTHUR
        (Silent as if waiting for
        Ruth to reply, then
        hesitantly answering, as
        if someone must respond)
        Scared.

DIRECTOR
Why?

ALISON MCARTHUR
It was a big loud noise.

RUTH DUFFY
It was the biggest loud noise!

ALISON MCARTHUR
It was louder than a crisp-bag clap!

DIRECTOR
Ha! And what was your first impulse? Did you want to rush out and see it, or did you want to run away and hide?

ALISON MCARTHUR
I can't remember.

RUTH DUFFY
Me neither.

DIRECTOR
That's like … Dali. The treachery of memory. Or … I think I'm mixing that up.

RUTH DUFFY
What's tarchery?

> DIRECTOR
> What you trust deliberately destroys that trust.

> RUTH DUFFY
> We trusted the corridor.

EXT. LAKE - TWILIGHT

Scene of shimmering water. Restful.

EXT. DRUMLIN - MORNING

Scene of sun rising above the rolling grassy hill. Birds sing.

EXT. MOBILE CLASSROOM - DAY

Finbar Adams climbs a ladder to check the guttering on a green mobile.

> DIRECTOR
> How did it affect you, the collapse of the corridor?

> FINBAR ADAMS
> Eh?

DIRECTOR
Did you feel a sense of doom? Or was it ... liberating, maybe?

FINBAR ADAMS
I thought of going in that office and telling Mrs Skerritt what I thought of her.

DIRECTOR
You thought she was to blame.

FINBAR ADAMS
A wain could've got hurt.

DIRECTOR
Did you think it was your fault too?

FINBAR ADAMS
Aye, could've told her what I thought of her before it happened.

DIRECTOR
That's interesting, telling someone what you think of them. I try to get people to tell me what they think of themselves.

FINBAR ADAMS
Aye.

DIRECTOR
Sometimes I wonder if this is the right line of work for me.

FINBAR ADAMS
Right.

DIRECTOR
How does the guttering look?

FINBAR ADAMS
Clear enough. Not the best though, gettin brittle. They're not new these mobiles. Came from another school that didn't need em. Willnae last two years.

DIRECTOR
You've told me before you think these kids are going to be stuck here longer than that.

FINBAR ADAMS
Aye. No-one gives ae fuck.

DIRECTOR
Not even the board of directors?

FINBAR ADAMS
Nah. Sure the priest has eight parishes.

DIRECTOR
Everyone is overstretched these days. Or perhaps I am wrong. Do you, Finbar, feel comfortable? Is there anything else you'd want to be?

FINBAR ADAMS
What like?

DIRECTOR
Well, like, say, a foreman. You said you'd worked on building sites before. Plenty of money in construction.

FINBAR ADAMS
I was a joiner once.

DIRECTOR
Oh really? Why'd you stop?

FINBAR ADAMS
Ah, it was a long time ago.

INT. MOBILE CLASSROOM - DAY

P4 classroom. Children listening to a lesson from Miss Donaghy. The sound is muted, as if coming from underwater. View of whole room, children listening. Then close-ups of individuals. Camera has slow bobbing movements as if on a wave. Tight on ANDY MCINTYRE chewing on the end of a pencil. Cut to TREVOR MCGEE who has an intent, scowling look of concentration. Cut to ORLAGH KEEGAN who has bright eyes and listening to the teacher with interest and pleasure. Cut to FIONA MCALEESE who is looking anxiously to the side out a window. Cut to BRONAGH WARD looking sad. Cut to Ruth Duffy whose flecked green and brown eyes seem to harbour the depths of all the oceans. Cut to Ali McArthur who is licking her lips as if they have become dry with the tension. Cut to JENNY BURNS who is nervously fidgeting in her seat. Cut to SEB DOUGLAS looking self-satisfied. Cut to GARRET TRAINER who has a mournful expression and is long and lanky. Cut to Daphne Donaghy who conducts the lesson with a wistful expression as if this is autumn heading into winter. Cut to full classroom, all the children, slow wave-like bobbing of the frame.

EXT. PLAYGROUND

Timelapse of swings and climbing frame, night following day, clouds flicking across the sky, wind occasionally jerking the swing from vertical.

INT. MOBILE CLASSROOM - DAY

Finbar Adams bleeding a radiator. It hisses.

> Sometimes I dream about chopping down the swings and the climbing frame. I lodge the axe into the timber support, then wake up.

DIRECTOR
Finbar?

FINBAR ADAMS
Yes?

DIRECTOR
Did you just speak, or was it the sound of the radiator hissing?

FINBAR ADAMS
I cannae mind saying anything.

                    DIRECTOR
          Ok …

EXT. PLAYGROUND - DAY

Swings slowly topple and fall. Wind whistles.

INT. ROAD - DAY

Shot of Ruth and Ali reaching the school. The school is a collection of mobiles in a field. They pause and wait for the Director to catch up with them.

                    DIRECTOR
          Thanks. Now, we've
          arrived at the school
          just as we arrive at an
          important part in our
          story.

                    RUTH DUFFY
          What story?

                    DIRECTOR
          The story of your old
          school. The moment when
          you first realised there
          was something wrong.

                    RUTH DUFFY
          I always knew there was
          something wrong.

DIRECTOR
How?

RUTH DUFFY
There were ghosts in the school.

ALISON MCARTHUR
There were no ghosts.

RUTH DUFFY
There were too ghosts. I saw them. You didn't see them because you were too scared to see them.

DIRECTOR
So you can only see ghosts if you aren't scared of seeing them?

RUTH DUFFY
Have you ever seen one?

DIRECTOR
Not since I grew up.

RUTH DUFFY
That's why. You're too scared. I'm not scared though.

DIRECTOR
Why not?

RUTH DUFFY
Jack the Ripper was my great great grandfather.

ALISON MCARTHUR
You said you were born from the Sun!

RUTH DUFFY
Yes, but he was Mama's great-great-great-great-grandfather.

DIRECTOR
I don't understand the Jack the Ripper connection. How does that help you see ghosts?

RUTH DUFFY
Jack the Ripper was a ghost. Spring-heeled Jack.

DIRECTOR
Spring-heeled Jack … now wait, you're mixing two things … no, actually. I understand. The ghost in you can see the ghosts. And your heritage, of scary monsters, renders you impervious to fear.

ALISON MCARTHUR
You never told me about ghosts.

RUTH DUFFY
I did all the time! Except when we weren't speaking. Maybe that's it.

ALISON MCARTHUR
I saw ghosts in the old houses, but not in the school.

DIRECTOR
What old houses?

ALISON MCARTHUR
Old houses up in the fields.

DIRECTOR
Ah. Where did all those people go?

RUTH DUFFY
The school ghost had a long droopy moustache.

DIRECTOR
Oh, it was a man? And was he in a big sheet?

> RUTH DUFFY
> No. A suit and tie and a hat.

> DIRECTOR
> What did he say to you?

> RUTH DUFFY
> He didn't say. He just waved. He looked a little sad.

> DIRECTOR
> And then what?

> RUTH DUFFY
> Disappeared.

INT. MOBILE CLASSROOM - DAY

MISS MCTAGGART sitting upright in a chair, hands in her lap, looking as if she is made of iron.

> DIRECTOR
> How long have you been a P3 teacher?

> MISS MCTAGGART
> (Glassy stare)
> I'll pretend you didn't ask that.

                    DIRECTOR
(Scared)
That's fine. Can you tell
me what you were doing
when the first jolt came?

                MISS MCTAGGART
We were praying to God.

                    DIRECTOR
What else?

                MISS MCTAGGART
(Icily)
What else?

                    DIRECTOR
Oh, sorry. Of course,
nothing else was
necessary.

                MISS MCTAGGART
(Silence)

                    DIRECTOR
Daphne Donaghy came in
and warned you that the
children needed to get
under the tables.

                MISS MCTAGGART
She has her head screwed
on, that woman.

> DIRECTOR
> You approve, then, of Miss Donaghy? I feel a strong collegiate bond between you.
>
> MISS MCTAGGART
> (Makes no motion to confirm or deny)
>
> DIRECTOR
> And what did you think, when she came in and told you that?
>
> MISS MCTAGGART
> I think you need to go and prepare better questions young lady.

Director's notes
Interviewing Miss McTaggart was one of the most terrifying moments for me. I felt as if at any moment I was going to be sent out for misbehaving. I suppose I was.

INT. SUPERMARKET – DAY

Daphne Donaghy moving round supermarket with a wire mesh basket.

> DAPHNE DONAGHY
> Out of fusilli. God I dislike penne.

DIRECTOR
Why?

DAPHNE DONAGHY
Why do you ask?

DIRECTOR
I'm trying to gain insight into your character.

DAPHNE DONAGHY
And discovering my reason for preferring one pasta shape over another is the way to do that?

DIRECTOR
I'm just trying to latch on.

DAPHNE DONAGHY
Interesting turn of phrase that. Like an infant, needing to latch on.

DIRECTOR
Hey, that's interesting. Maybe that reveals my own insecurity about this project. I keep thinking it's all going to end in failure.

DAPHNE DONAGHY
So you're worried about how this shoot is going.

DIRECTOR
I've not directed a project yet I didn't think was doomed.

DAPHNE DONAGHY
Then it's a good sign that you're anxious.

DIRECTOR
Possibly. All I know is that I have to film. I have to ask questions and hope it somehow works out.

DAPHNE DONAGHY
Does it often work out?

DIRECTOR
Well, let's see. I've made three attempts at feature directing. Two of them were ok. One didn't work at all. I'm still not sure why.

DAPHNE DONAGHY
66% success is good.

> DIRECTOR
> Yeah but I'm still lacking that moment. You know what I mean. The moment when someone opens up.

> DAPHNE DONAGHY
> Maybe we've healed. The wound has closed over.

> DIRECTOR
> I've been thinking about that. Like water beneath a still lake.

INT. PRINCIPAL'S OFFICE - DAY

SUSAN SKERRITT is sitting behind her large desk. The room is dim, the windows are tinted and there are tasteful venetian blinds which are three-quarters closed.

> DIRECTOR
> When did you have a sense that something was wrong?

> SUSAN SKERRITT
> You have to understand that the layout of the former school was such that we were quite far removed from the lower

wing. We heard and saw nothing at all.

>   DIRECTOR

Some of the Primary Seven children claim they heard it beginning –

>   SUSAN SKERRITT

Oh, I think you'll find children will claim they know everything all the time. But I assure you, the unusual layout of our school –

>   DIRECTOR

Why did the school have such an unusual layout? From what I understand, it was two buildings joined by a corridor.

>   SUSAN SKERRITT

There was an extension of the school in the 1980s.

>   DIRECTOR

Yes, but why so remote from the main body of the school? The Google Map images I have from a year ago show it ten or fifteen metres distant.

SUSAN SKERRITT
Well, that was before my time. But my understanding is that that was the only natural place for it to go or excavation into a hill would have been required.

DIRECTOR
It is quite a hilly round here, isn't it?

SUSAN SKERRITT
The upper part of the school is – was – situated on a high spot, flat. But the lower part of the school lies at the base of a ring of drumlins.

DIRECTOR
Must have had terrible problems with damp.

SUSAN SKERRITT
That's why the boiler room was situated in the lower half. Our heating bill was somewhat enormous, I agree. Those high sloping ceilings did not make things much better.

                    DIRECTOR
          High   sloping   ceilings.
          Yes,   I've   seen   the
          photos.

                    SUSAN SKERRITT
          (rising)
          Any   further   questions
          just let me know.

Director's notes
Did I have any more questions for Mrs Skerritt? Were all my questions actually for myself? I couldn't think. There was something about her sepia-tinted windows and mahogany brown desk and dark decor that rendered me as depressed as the hollow wherein the ill-fated lower wing of the school had been built. Or perhaps … to reverse the metaphor … I had dried up. Always the chief dread, when engaged on creative enterprise. You can only hope that inspiration comes.

INT. DUFFY LIVINGROOM – EVENING

Ruth Duffy sits alone on sofa, twiddling her thumbs.

                    DIRECTOR
          What   was   going   through
          your mind at that point?

RUTH DUFFY
I thought it was a nirthquake. But it wasn't as much fun.

DIRECTOR
Was it noisy?

RUTH DUFFY
The janitor was making a lot of noise next door. He wanted to knock down the Primary Three classroom.

DIRECTOR
Why was he doing that?

RUTH DUFFY
To make it fall over.

DIRECTOR
Did you think he was rescuing you?

RUTH DUFFY
I thought he liked breaking things like the corridor.

DIRECTOR
He says it was Mrs Skerritt's fault.

RUTH DUFFY
I didn't see Mrs Skerritt there but maybe she came in at night. But I was in the classroom when it fell so I maybe I didn't see her.

DIRECTOR
No, I mean the janitor says she just let it happen. It would have happened anyway, just by nobody stopping it.

RUTH DUFFY
Do Mama and Papa stop this house falling over?

DIRECTOR
Yes … in the sense that if they noticed something wrong they would get someone in to fix it. Mrs Skerritt didn't do that, says the Janitor.

RUTH DUFFY
But the P3 classroom needed help to fall over. Why did the Janitor do that?

> DIRECTOR
> Well that's the question, isn't it. I'm afraid he's not very articulate.
>
> RUTH DUFFY
> I know about Articulate. You have to guess all the words in two minutes.
>
> DIRECTOR
> Maybe you're right. I just need to give him more time. Let him tell it his way.
>
> RUTH DUFFY
> I need to go to bed.

DOWN THE MINE (PART II)

'I'd advise you, Thomas, to put more woomph into that pick,' said McKnicken, supervising the digging of the hole. 'Elbert, fill them buckets with spadewater. All right. Another hour then take a rest. I'm going to the brickies to see if they can throw us a few hundred this after.'

The main shaft sank slowly to completion. A great chamber three yards in circumference, it journeyed six hundred yards into the depths of the Earth. Two seams had been discovered separated by an impervious shale bed a few yards thick. The potential yield was estimated to be bounteous.

'A fine pit, gentlemen!' toasted Houldsworth-Farrington. 'Now tell me: when shall these riches be mine?'

McKnicken allowed the surveyor to explain, interpreting the surveyor when he became too wordsome. Houldsworth-Farrington seemed willing to toast any new term he had not heard before and by the end of the explanation had to be carried to bed.

And so the Houldsworth-Farrington Mine was opened.

Elbert had a mad yearn to be on the town–so away he went, him and another two lads. They begged a lift off the back of a trailer heading that way.

'Where're ye headed for exactly?' asked the red-faced driver.

'Docks,' came Elbert's somewhat cagey response. His companions, Stephen McSonder and wee Rick, grinned at him.

'The Docks, heh?' asked the driver, as if it weren't really a question, and laughed.

They arrived stiff from the journey. A sawdust-covered establishment, they spent a few on frothy mixtures. A group of musicians were setting up in the corner. Elbert went over to sit near them. He liked a bit of music. He chatted to the fiddle man between numbers.

Soon enough McSonder was trying to get up and dance but a bit sozzled and laughter so Rick and Elbert lured him out of the way in the corner with the promise of more ale. The drinking continued till darkness had fallen. Candlelight led the way. There was fog of the mind that hid the self from the self so that it knew not what it wanted. But it did know great excitement and the carnal lusts of the flesh. And the ladies were so arranged as to be irresistible. There was one with soft skin and beautiful eyes that Elbert had liked once before. In this room and having difficulty with getting his trousers off he laughed and she laughed and he felt dizzy but on the bed and with his rough calloused hands on her it felt good after a week of shoveling dirt to be juicing it in the squalor of his own filthy ardour. Filling the soft-skinned one with his joy and wetting her lips with his own soft lips and the hardness of his joy with hard movements spilling away like stars alighting distantly he shuddered and grabbed her tight up around the back with the dress she hadn't fully taken off and loved her. He held her and felt the relief of it and the love of it and tried to ward off the shame that always came with him holding her tight but there was the knowledge that he'd have not do it again but wanting to put it away from him like a soggy blanket but he was always doing it again and again and he knew he'd always do it. If his Mama knew, the shame. He dragged his pants up and shoveled a few coins out and wandered downstairs into the night to watch the clouds expose the weak moon in the oily waters of the dark docks by the quays.

Thomas called from the fence over the field near her house. This was a spot where her parents wouldn't see him easily, although he suspected they could and always had. Talks were hard with 'em. They'd consented though. Little choice.

    He gave another shrill whistle like a blackbird hiding in the briars. Patricia's head appeared at the door. She disappeared again. Then she was out in the garden and walking towards him.

    'Thomas!' she said.

    He tried to keep the grin off his face and failed.

    'Hay little rose-bud. And what about the wee wun? What kind of a name is it goina have?'

    He glanced towards the house before giving Patricia a quick, swift kiss on the lips. He wanted more but supposed it might be a bit time before he could do that again. He scowled.

    'How's your'uns?' he asked. 'And the others ... the sisters ...'

'Don't you pretend you don't know their names.'

'Maybe I know their names or maybe I don't care.'

'I'd better go in.'

Thomas was annoyed. 'Why better you go in? What's wrong with out here? Do I smell of the pit?' Thomas inspected the odour of his clothes, and then coughed.

Patricia laughed. 'Of course you smell. But that's not the reason. I've duties.'

'*I'm* your duty,' he said.

She kissed him on the nose and then, with evident sadness, returned home.

He watched her go, a sour expression on his face, then turned to go himself. Back home to that small cottage with his mother, father, two brothers and a sister. And where soon-to-be-wife would presently join. How on *Earth* was there space for that? He kicked a clod and sent it flying. It would not be the pleasures of the flesh to be assembled in those close quarters for who knew how long. He needed his own place. He might save enough for one a year from now. Near the stream. He wanted to wake and see kingfishers. A year. Aye, they could wait a year. It was long hours; but when McKnicken told you how many hundredweight you'd delivered, and when he counted out the monies, and added a wee bit to help you–well, that was all right. Though Thomas didn't like hanging above the big six hundred yard drop in that tin can. That bucket that went up to the shoulder and a lid on top and you had to hang on tight to the chains and not move while two lads winched you down in the morning. Being down there was fine. But then back up in that blasted can in the eve. At the start you'd be all right but half way you'd be swinging side to side in the dark thinking that that was it and if you didna get bashed against the walls you'd just tip out and they'd have to take you out of there in pieces.

Next morning he did exactly that. Down he went. He could tell he was near the bottom by the change in sound, which seemed to open out, and just as quickly that juddering yank through his legs near jarring them off and he falling out of the barrel–he cursed the ones above for yet another shit-slide down.

He lit his lamp, expert at it now in the dark, and gave a loud whistle for them to hoist it up so Elbert, if he'd arrived yet, could come down too.

```
INT. MOBILE CLASSROOM - DAY
Daphne Donaghy in empty classroom. Sounds
of children shouting and playing outside.

                    DIRECTOR
          And  where  were  you
          standing?

                    DAPHNE DONAGHY
          In a door frame.

                    DIRECTOR
          What was it like?

                    DAPHNE DONAGHY
          Maybe a bit like hitting
          a car when you're trying
          to  park  in  a  busy
          supermarket. You  know
          you've  hit  it,  but you
          aren't sure how bad it is
          and  you  can  still  fool
          yourself  that  maybe  it
          didn't happen.
```

DIRECTOR
You thought it was your imagination?

DAPHNE DONAGHY
Not at all. It was very real. But together with the certainty that it had happened came the denial that it was happening.

DIRECTOR
Were you aware that you were fighting against a denial in yourself?

DAPHNE DONAGHY
Oh yes.

DIRECTOR
Some of the children have told me that they wanted to jump up and run outside. I'm surprised that didn't happen.

DAPHNE DONAGHY
Children are like adults in groups. They can equally well become braver or more terrified. Like a flock of sheep. Which I suppose makes me a sheepdog.

INT. BOILER ROOM - DAY

Finbar Adams rolling a rollie when suddenly there is a cracking sound from without. He drops his rollie and stands up quickly, an angry expression on his face. Then he collects himself and sits back down. He thinks for a minute, then starts rummaging in his tools for something.

>   DIRECTOR
> What were you looking for?

>   FINBAR ADAMS
> I was looking for this: a torch.

>   DIRECTOR
> A torch? Why?

>   FINBAR ADAMS
> Well, if you don't know what's going to happen, you're sometimes best getting a torch. Other tools you can make out of each other, or whatever is lying around, but only one thing's a torch, and that's a torch.

DIRECTOR
And what were you thinking?

FINBAR ADAMS
Nothing. I was just getting the torch. Wasn't thinking anything else.

DIRECTOR
Funny, a couple of people have told me that. That they weren't thinking, they were doing. Or thinking without thoughts.

FINBAR ADAMS
Aye.

DIRECTOR
Once you had the torch, what did you do?

FINBAR ADAMS
I picked up my toolbag. Went to the corridor.

DIRECTOR
And what did you see?

FINBAR ADAMS
Saw nothin different there.

THE COLLAPSE CONTINUES

Finbar Adams stood at the site of the fallen corridor, blocked off now behind plasterboard. There was another distinct 'crack' somewhere behind him. From the Primary Three or Four wing of the school. He wheeled round, frightened.

He went directly to the boiler room and turned off every stop-cock he could find. Then, with a large L-shaped metal rod, he went outside and opened a hatch in the ground. He turned off the water supply for the school. Round the corner was an enormously capacious school oil storage tank; he rotated the stop-cock on this. It all took a matter of minutes. He returned to the school. He had just stepped inside when the entire building jolted as if a fire-cracker had been lit under it.

'Fuck!' he said. He dropped his torch.

Picking the torch back up, he shone it on his hand to check it still worked. He noticed his hand was shaking. He knocked on the Primary Three classroom and entered without waiting for invitation.

Initially the classroom seemed empty to him. Then he noticed the ancient one, Miss McTaggart, glowering at him from the storeroom doorway. Almost the same instant he noticed wains cowering under the tables.

'Aye, good,' he said, and left, carefully clicking the door shut behind him.

He was going nextdoor to the Primary Four school room when the bottom fell out of his stomach. He tumbled awkwardly against the floor.

'Ah, shite!' he cried. It was his ankle. He'd only gone and twisted it.

THE COLLAPSE CONTINUES

Crack. Another shoot through the descent. The walls and ceiling remain intact. The children sing animal songs. Miss Donaghy wisely threatened them first with times-tables questions, so that they were more malleable. In the next room the Primary Threes obediently intone the lord's prayer.

Another jolt, and the journey into the belly of the whale continues. It strikes Daphne Donaghy that, like Jonah, somehow they are surviving. What are the odds of that continuing? The floor shivers beneath her feet. Finbar shrieks and curses somewhere in the corridor. She instructs the children to continue their song while she finds out what has happened to the janitor.

She reaches the door. She notices a thin hairline fracture in the shatterproof glass. She glances behind her at the classroom windows and sees that the horizon is now two feet above its normal location. She turns back and steps out into the corridor. She is thrown to the ground. Pain fires up her elbow. The children scream and holler. She shouts that times-tables are coming if they don't behave themselves: they must keep holding onto the table legs. The janitor comes over to help her up. She shoos him away. She remarks that she came out to help him up not the other way round. He helps her up anyway, complaining about things she doesn't understand. They go into the classroom together, but separately. Miss Donaghy goes to the storeroom doorway and Finbar Adams stands the middle of the room staring out the window. She says to him to get into a doorway. He barely gives her a glance as he walks back out again. She curses him for the sore arm she pointlessly suffered on his behalf. It is half past two in the afternoon, the clock on the wall says. Regular chanting continues from the P3 classroom behind her.

Finbar Adams comes back in looking grave. He says he's going to be in the P3 classroom awhile. She asks him why. He says something about the girder truss. She asks him if the Primary Threes are in danger. He says aye. She goes into the Primary Three classroom and as she enters another enormous shock hurtles her to the floor.

THE COLLAPSE CONTINUES

Miss Donaghy picked herself up, unsteadily. Children behind her screaming, children in front of her screaming. The floor had a distinct slope now.

'Miss McTaggart,' said Miss Donaghy, 'these children need to go into the Primary Four classroom.'

Miss McTaggart immediately commanded the children to stand up, put their chairs in and walk in single file into the P4 classroom with fingers on lips. Thirty seconds later the children had filed through to the other room. Miss Donaghy felt herself in awe at Miss McTaggart's authority.

At the back of the room, Finbar Adams was waving his hand in front of him, fingers pinched together, inspecting the ceiling as if trying to gauge the length of the screwdriver he was going to need. Miss Donaghy left him to it.

'Children, allow the Primary Threes to bunch up next to you under the desks. Make space. No, not over there. Stay under these two desks near the door.' She didn't want them near Andy McIntyre, who was liable to punch anyone (other than Garret Trainer) in a stressful situation like this.

She turned to Miss McTaggart. 'Get the children occupied,' said this elderly teacher.

Get the children occupied. By God, how small they all are. Get them to sing more songs. Why does only Happy Birthday come to mind? Need a call and response one. We could sing some hymn, but I don't think I could deal with that.

Another lurch. The kids screamed like alarumed blackbirds. And it seemed to Miss Donaghy that the floor had developed another degree of southwards tilt. The Titanic came to mind.

'Right, spelling,' shouted Miss Donaghy. 'P3s say the hardest words they can think of. P4s have to spell them. Shout them out!'

She had to repeat her command several times, and Miss McTaggart reinforcing it in a strict no-nonsense tone, before the children began doing it. It took the fun out of it but, Miss Donaghy realised, fun was only going to be achieved with great difficulty in the present context.

She heard sawing from next door. She wondered what on Earth Finbar was up to.


```
INT. BOILER ROOM - DAY

Finbar collecting together a can of paint
and a paint brush.

                FINBAR ADAMS
          I left it in the turps.

                DIRECTOR
          How has life been? Are
          you trying to reassemble
          the pieces?

                FINBAR ADAMS
          What?
```

DIRECTOR
Since the collapse. I mean, there's this thing that Freud calls … can't remember the quote. That's going to make me look stupid.

FINBAR ADAMS
I've bin keepin myself busy.

DIRECTOR
Painting?

FINBAR ADAMS
No, this is only the first bout of painting. But ye see these mobiles they just took em from some other school that had built an extension, they're nat new. So they need a lick. Let's go.

Finbar Adams tracks out over fields towards a mobile.

DIRECTOR
Whose mobile is this?

FINBAR ADAMS
Headteacher's. Wonder who'll be now. Hope Daphne but sure.

DIRECTOR
What?

FINBAR ADAMS
I said, Hope Daphne, but sure she'll be retiring.

DIRECTOR
What do you mean? Has Mrs Skerritt gone?

FINBAR ADAMS
(turns to camera, with a broad smile on his face). Sure, you don't know?

DIRECTOR
Know what?

FINBAR ADAMS
Ach! It's the best … Ah, now. Here was me thinking ye were the all-seeing eye.

DIRECTOR
I've never said that. Actually my whole schtick is sort of to show up the limited and … what's the word. Fuck, my mind really is dead today. Anyway, tell me the news. Falsifiable? No, that's not the word.

FINBAR ADAMS
Aye, I know that annoying cannae find the word thing. Then you're makin your dinner and the doorbell rings and you remember. It'll come.

DIRECTOR
Yes. Doesn't make good TV. Anyway. Tell me the news.

FINBAR ADAMS
Aye. She's gone away off. Had to of a sudden. And you know who else has just been put away off? I mean, had to go to another parish?

DIRECTOR
(pause)
What? You serious?

FINBAR ADAMS
(With relish)
Aye.

DIRECTOR
That's incredible. How did I miss this? That would have been ... maybe not relevant, but the drama ... I knew I should have come in last week. I

had this job on a documentary about rats in a Kildare warehouse. Damn!

                    FINBAR ADAMS
          Been the talk, let me
          tell you. Except no-one's
          suppose to be talking
          about it.

                    DIRECTOR
          Wow. So this mobile is
          empty. Why are you
          painting it then?

                    FINBAR ADAMS
          I guess I just like to
          remind myself she's gone.
          She was an oul ****.

INT. MOBILE CLASSROOM - DAY

Children all sitting about, busy gluing things together and playing with pens and being creative.

                    DIRECTOR
          I've noticed that there
          is a real ebb and flow to
          the day, a rhythm, like
          the tides. Between noise
          and peace. You do this
          deliberately?

DAPHNE DONAGHY
Some children like noise, some like quiet. I try to guide them through the day so we get a bit of both. Quiet for the abstract learning then let a bit of energy escape, then a bit of quiet learning again and tease that out as far as possible until breaktime. Then they wreck themselves outside and honestly I'm pretty much done by then as well. I usually give up on serious education about an hour before lunch.

DIRECTOR
It seems to work. Do you notice any differences in the class, compared to the way it was?

DAPHNE DONAGHY
Oh yes. Only last week poor Ali burst in tears and I made the error of bringing her up to the front thinking I'd be able to calm her down and get to teaching again. But soon the whole room was in floods. I should

have known that would happen.

                DIRECTOR
God damn – excuse my language. How'd I miss that? Of all the weeks I take off. I should give you the camera.

                DAPHNE DONAGHY
I'm not sure I'd be able to video the emotional bits. My instinct would be to turn the camera off.

                DIRECTOR
I have the same impulse, honestly. You know, I sometimes think this isn't the job for me. I don't have the killer instinct.

                DAPHNE DONAGHY
Trevor, don't use the pencil that way. You know what I'm talking about. Why don't you draw me a nice picture of Bozo?

                DIRECTOR
Who's Bozo?

DAPHNE DONAGHY
Trevor's dog. Very undisciplined dog. Possibly the thing Trevor likes most in the universe.

DIRECTOR
He's drawing very enthusiastically now. You know these children so well. Are you going to go for the Principal's position?

DAPHNE DONAGHY
Good God no. I'm retiring, don't you remember?

DIRECTOR
Yes. Just thought you'd be interested in it. Everyone seems to mention you in connection with it.

DAPHNE DONAGHY
That's very flattering. But I think I need to stop doing this. Not that I know what I'm doing after … I keep wondering. Maybe …

                    DIRECTOR
            What?

            (fight breaks out in
            corner of classroom,
            between Seb and Ruth)

                 DAPHNE DONAGHY
            Hey! None of that!
            (Sorts fight out,
            separates children. Talks
            to them. Waves at camera
            in a gesture that plainly
            says "turn it off")
            We'll talk later.

Director's notes
My original idea had been to unpick the effect that the collapse had had on the internal lives of those involved. But it looked like their lives were going on much as before. Then I got this call. Bernie Gardner, a contact in the agency, said he'd shown it to the Board. But then he said he didn't think there was much chance of my getting any funding to reenact the collapse or the Victorian salt mine stuff. And meanwhile here was me drinking too much with my friends while trying to raise a two-year old and trying to maintain a freelance documentary career while making ends meet doing odd jobs in the film industry at weird hours like weekends and evenings. I was beginning to wonder if this whole film wasn't really about me in some kind of deep way, like the way Herzog's films are all about him. I've been trying to separate myself from Herzog because his influence weighs too heavily on me. I see no point in simply reenacting him. Of course,

that would be interesting in itself, but not the kind of thing I really wanted to be doing. In common with Herzog I wanted to get to the deeper reality, ideally in a way that compromised verisimilitude. The reality on this shoot seemed to be so palpable I couldn't work with it. The school had collapsed; people were recovering in their own ways; there was fear that there would be another collapse, even though the outlines of the mine had now been definitively mapped. My life was some kind of inquiry that was never going to get finished. I kept wondering whether I should be looking at the mechanics of my investigation, whether that was a route for me, but the whole project was already so time-consuming I didn't want to be ploughing through *more* extraneous matter ... keep the focus, keep it on the people. On excavating them, going deeper. Down and down for the good turf. I had no idea how to dig, it was beginning to dawn on me. I'd taken along the right equipment, but there was an art to putting your coarse boot on the lug. I also kept wondering why adversity wasn't making me more and more determined to conquer. Perhaps I had nothing to prove. Perhaps it was *I* who had collapsed and not the school. If I was the subject I could not be the director. In that case someone else had to point the camera and ask the questions. Yes – what an idea! I decided to ask Ruth Duffy.

EXT. SCHOOL PLAYGROUND - DAY

Director is sitting on a swing, smiling at the camera uneasily, as if Ruth, operating the camera, might press a combination of buttons that rendered the camera inert.

DIRECTOR
Ok? You're sure that you can do it?

RUTH DUFFY
I can see you on the swing. And there's a little timer on the bottom.

DIRECTOR
That's good, it means it's running. Now don't press the red button until you want it to stop.

RUTH DUFFY
There's two red buttons.

DIRECTOR
That's ok. It's the big red button. If you can't find it just ask and I will. Now. Ask me tough questions, and if I don't answer them ask me them again. And of course remember to ask me how I feel.

RUTH DUFFY
Ok. Why are you on the swing?

DIRECTOR

I … That's a good question. A really good question. I think I was trying to depict myself as a young girl, naive, inexperienced. Perhaps as a way of going back into myself, to find out what happened to those wellsprings of creativity that seem now to have irrevocably dried up.

RUTH DUFFY
What does 'erveobcly' mean?

DIRECTOR
Irrevocably.

RUTH DUFFY
Errovacbly.

DIRECTOR
That's it. Honestly I don't know. I thought I did. Well. Ok. It means … that you can't do anything about it.

RUTH DUFFY
Why not?

DIRECTOR
Wow. You are ten times better than me. I might

get you to direct the rest of the film.

RUTH DUFFY
Why can't you do anything about it?

DIRECTOR
Too good … Um. Because I'm lazy. Shallow. Just want a comfortable life. But that's me blaming myself, as indeed I've been trained to do by society. But why should I be the victim? What good does it do? I could play music. I used to play guitar and sing. I like to write songs when I can. It's been about five years since I wrote a song, can you believe that? But do you know the best thing about being a singer-songwriter instead of a freelance documentary maker?

RUTH DUFFY
What does "freelans" mean?

DIRECTOR
Freelance means no-one pays you until you've

>   done all the work and
>   they like it and if no-
>   one likes it then you've
>   spent a year of your life
>   and half your own
>   savings.
>
>   RUTH DUFFY
>   Are your savings your
>   money?
>
>   DIRECTOR
>   Not any more they aren't.
>
>   RUTH DUFFY
>   Are you going to starve?
>
>   DIRECTOR
>   (Pause)
>   Well, I can't eat
>   expensive video editing
>   software, that's for
>   sure. But no, I'll at
>   least be able to eat.

INT. WALL - DAY

Shot of a brick wall. Brief rasping sound. Another brief rasping sound. Then a regular back-and-forth, and sawdust starts to fall, like snow, past the brick wall. Then the sound of a snap and a plank of wood falls down. Sound of wood hitting ground. Cut to still image of plank lying on the ground in a ring of sawdust.

INT. BOILER ROOM - DAY

Finbar Adams is displaying a saw to the camera.

>   DIRECTOR
>   That's the saw?

>   FINBAR ADAMS
>   Aye.

>   DIRECTOR
>   Remarkable. It is like
>   seeing an object from the
>   Titanic.

>   FINBAR ADAMS
>   Aye.

>   DIRECTOR
>   How'd you feel as you
>   were sawing the wood?

>   FINBAR ADAMS
>   Gave me something to do.

>   DIRECTOR
>   Did it take long?

>   FINBAR ADAMS
>   Minute or two.

DIRECTOR
What made you think you needed to start sawing?

FINBAR ADAMS
Should've done it in the bloomin' corridor, could see the thing was going to coup. Didn't let myself. Still annoyed about it. Twas Mrs Skerritt's fault.

DIRECTOR
Perhaps her being separated from your wing of the school liberated you from her inhibitory presence?

FINBAR ADAMS
Aye.

DIRECTOR
(Maintains a silence)

FINBAR ADAMS
Aye. Started thinkin straight. Like, the load on that girder truss, was goin to snap like, and bruise the wains on the head.

DIRECTOR
Wow.

FINBAR ADAMS
So Miss McTaggart and Miss Donaghy rounded up the Primary Three wains and shepherded them into that Primary Four room. Then I could get at it with the saw and good thing I did too.

DIRECTOR
Yes, good thing, given what happened next.

FINBAR ADAMS
Aye, the whole thing was gonna coup like a sleeping cow.

DIRECTOR
Like a cow?

FINBAR ADAMS
A tipped cow.

DIRECTOR
Tipped?

FINBAR ADAMS
Ach. I'm talkin about pushin it, like, when it's asleep.

DIRECTOR
I've never heard of that.

FINBAR ADAMS
No cows in Belfast. Here there's cows and what young'uns do after a feed of drink is tip a cow.

DIRECTOR
What happens to the cow?

FINBAR ADAMS
It tips over like, surprised.

DIRECTOR
That's unfortunate for the cow.

FINBAR ADAMS
Bit tight on the cow all right.

DIRECTOR
I guess we're all complicit in farmed animal cruelty.

FINBAR ADAMS
Aye.

DIRECTOR
And that's how you know that it was like tipping a cow.

FINBAR ADAMS
That's it.

EXT. WATER - DAY

Pool of water, undisturbed. Cut to still image of plank of wood lying on the ground in a halo of sawdust. Then cut to pool of water. Plank of wood splashes violently into it, shattering the image of peace and serenity.

INT. DARKNESS - NIGHT

Glitters in the darkness; or these may be the imagination of the viewer. Slow footsteps. These sound like they are in an interior space that may be vast or may be tightly enclosed. There is a crunching sound as if of gravel or rocksalt.

THE COLLAPSE CONTINUES

It was by this time three in the afternoon. Parents began to arrive to pick up their children. The first parents to arrive were Elizabeth and Padraig Duffy.

INT. LIVINGROOM - DAY

ELIZABETH DUFFY and PADRAIG DUFFY in their livingroom. Padraig Duffy is sitting on an armchair: a young man, in his early thirties, bright-eyed, looks like a bit of a messer. Dynamic and animated in his movements. Wants to say everything at once. To his right sits Elizabeth Duffy, also early thirties, looking more anxious and perhaps irritated.

                    PADRAIG DUFFY
          It was really weird. At
          first I couldn't believe
          it.

                    DIRECTOR
          How was it?

                    PADRAIG DUFFY
          Well, there was this hole
          in the ground. Great big
          hole. And the lower half
          of the school was
          disappearing into it.

                    ELIZABETH DUFFY
          We didn't see that at
          first. We were at the
          front of the school, the
          upper half.

                    PADRAIG DUFFY
          We wait there normally.
          The bell rings at ten
          past, I think, and out
          come some of the older
          ones.

ELIZABETH DUFFY
The younger children have left by 2pm.

PADRAIG DUFFY
The older ones came out. I remember thinking, "she's keeping them in late today." But then I remember thinking: "It's further to walk from down there." But then a couple of kids ran round into the playground, and then ran back saying something to one of the teachers.

ELIZABETH DUFFY
They were saying something about the lower half of the school.

PADRAIG DUFFY
I think they said about the swings first.

ELIZABETH DUFFY
And then that the lower half of the school had vanished.

PADRAIG DUFFY
Which was an exaggeration, because it had only really disappeared from view. If

they'd gone a little further –

    DIRECTOR
They'd have vanished into a hole.

    PADRAIG DUFFY
That's right. Where the lower half of the school was.

    ELIZABETH DUFFY
We waited for another few minutes. Whatever it was those kids had said to the teacher, she sent them off when their parents arrived, and didn't seem much concerned.

    DIRECTOR
Were you concerned?

    ELIZABETH DUFFY
No.

    PADRAIG DUFFY
It seemed normal. Kids are always talking shite about stuff.

    ELIZABETH DUFFY
We waited, but come twenty past there were no

Primary Fours or Threes out, so myself and Padraig went round the side of the school.

                PADRAIG DUFFY
We wouldn't normally do that but we'd both seen the P5 kids run over to the teacher and tell her the swings had disappeared, so I think we knew something was up.

                ELIZABETH DUFFY
Not that we thought exactly that way. But the strange thing is, the wait wasn't like that dread when you imagine something horrible to explain someone's lateness, like a car crash, or something like that. This was more like a certainty that something had happened, and a knowledge that we must deal with it, in whatever way that turned out to be.

                DIRECTOR
You felt this too, Padraig?

                    PADRAIG DUFFY
          I can't remember thinking
          anything, actually. I
          just remember me and Beth
          walking round without any
          real expectation.

                    DIRECTOR
          And when you saw what you
          saw?

                    PADRAIG DUFFY
          Well, it was bit of a
          shock.

                    ELIZABETH DUFFY
          The calm disappeared
          then. I didn't believe
          it. I had to try and stop
          myself panicking.

                    PADRAIG DUFFY
          Felt a bit freaked out.
          It was intense.

INT. WALL - DAY

Slow zoom into an analogue clock on a wall. Reads five past three.

Sound of hammering and chiseling and knocking.

THE COLLAPSE CONTINUES

Finbar Adams knew he had a sledgehammer somewhere. It was probably in the boiler room.

INT. WALL – DAY

More banging and sawing from some unseen location above. Sawdust falls. We zoom out and see Finbar Adams standing on a ladder. We zoom out more and see him stop and climb down, and then grin uneasily at the camera.

> FINBAR ADAMS
> Like that?

> DIRECTOR
> Only you know what it was like.

> FINBAR ADAMS
> Well it was like that, more or less. Sawing, hammering. Then I went and got the sledgehammer and started sledging at the base of the outside wall where the store cupboard was.

> DIRECTOR
> Why there?

FINBAR ADAMS
I didna know where to start. But it was wrong. I decided I'd bash a different bit. But needed to get up on the ladder and that wasn't handy. Place could heave ho at any minute and didna want to be falling off the cupboard with a ten pound sledge in me hands.

DIRECTOR
That how you got the bad back?

FINBAR ADAMS
Aye, when the thing did come and left me on the floor. Banged me head too. But the sledge at least didna hit me.

DIRECTOR
That was a relatively small lurch, wasn't it, the one that took you off the cupboards while you were trying to sledge the upper wall.

FINBAR ADAMS
Aye. But at this point I didna really know what I was at. Just had a sense

I needed to get the P3 room off from the P4. But sledging wasn't gonna work. Or not the random sledgin I was doin. Needed to stop and think about it.

              DIRECTOR
What you think about?

              FINBAR ADAMS
Didna think. Just looked at it. Floor was all slanting like and I was thinkin the whole roof was gonna cave in. Then I had to think like what the fuck is going on. It was like sinkin in a ship. You seen Titanic?

              DIRECTOR
Yes.

              FINBAR ADAMS
Know the bit where it sinks?

              DIRECTOR
I do remember that bit.

              FINBAR ADAMS
But no, the bit where it goes up in the air. You know, it's horizontal,

next thing that wee whelp is trying to climb up a deck that's stickin way up in the air because all the water was in the other end of the ship. Well, I kep thinking about all the water being down in the bottom end of the P3 classroom. And that didn' look good.

DIRECTOR
There was water?

FINBAR ADAMS
No yet, I'm saying it was like there was water. And we weren't going to just slide into the ocean, like, or the ground that was going like the ocean. We was going to snap in two. Or at least I thought that'd be a good way a do it. Snap us in two. But I didna know exactly where the snap would be. Centre gravity, you see. Gotta know where that is.

DIRECTOR
How did you figure it out?

FINBAR ADAMS
Well first I was thinking that I could move all the chairs and tables down the far side of the room. But then I thought, Finbar, you're absolutely full of shite because what weight are a couple chairs and tables? So then I said to myself, right, next thing you do is you make the place where it cracks. But got to work with where the crack actually is. So I had to figure out where the crack was before there was a crack.

DIRECTOR
That seems, if you don't mind my saying, a Herculean task; or even Quixotic.

FINBAR ADAMS
I dunno what quick-oats you talkin about.

DIRECTOR
Don Quixote, the hero of Cervantes' satire on chivalric romance. He tilts at windmills,

thinking they are giants.
And so on.

FINBAR ADAMS
Well, thon Quickoats might have been better in this situation. I was lookin and lookin and thinkin. Then I closed me eyes.

DIRECTOR
Closed them?

FINBAR ADAMS
Aye.

DIRECTOR
And what did you see?

FINBAR ADAMS
I think I saw darkness. And that's how I knew what was about te happen. I opened me eyes again.

DIRECTOR
And, opening your eyes, what revealed itself?

FINBAR ADAMS
It was that girder truss. I'd sawn it in the wrong place.

THE COLLAPSE CONTINUES

Cursing, Finbar Adams mounted the ladder in the middle of the room and scurried up it. But the slope of the ceiling was such that he couldn't reach it. The ceiling was too high. He'd need his big ladder, but was still in the boiler room. So he ran to go and get it.

RUTH DUFFY'S DIARY

Today I took a snail and Threuw it at Seb's head. He told off to me to Miss Donaghy and she Scolded me but I could tell she was secretely Glad.

DAPHNE DONAGHY'S JOURNAL

Well, here goes. I haven't kept a journal for about forty years. But retirement is impending so I'll give it a go. Retirement, retirement and retirement. What is one to do? I feel certain I've exhausted all my creative powers by drinking wine in front of mild TV entertainment four decades in a row. Of course, it could be me being lazy. Look at that Director, young, full of energy, raising a kid and trying to tell the story of whatever happened to us before and after the school sank into a pit. What am I going to do? I suppose I've always wanted to paint. But the energy ... my heart sinks. Even now. Even writing this. I said I'd write for thirty minutes. Three minutes have passed. I have twenty-seven minutes left. Twenty-six. Good God, what has happened to me? Outside, I am vibrant, I enthuse children. It is easy to enthuse children. You just pay attention to them. Who will pay attention to a grey-haired retiree? Milicent, Angela, Trudy. Not one of them genuinely interested in art. Am I genuinely interested in art? I always wanted to do it. Not just as a hobby. I feel acutely, if I don't do something serious, I'll have wasted my life. But it's ... I was going to say impossible. I know it isn't, in theory. But in practice it means mastering technique, which I've never got near started doing. And after that? Will I have served some useful function? I promised myself as an adolescent that no matter what I would paint and I would draw. Everyone keeps talking about ten thousand hours. Ten thousand hours, said Angela the other day: that's how long it takes to become a genius. How many hours is that per day for ten years? Here I am, testing my own mathematics as if I were a child. So that's how it feels: I really do not want to do the calculation. Ok, lets make it easy. Ten hours a day. A thousand days. That's about three years. Five hours a day, six years. Six years to get technically proficient. That makes it sound easy. Then four years left to do some real work–maybe it's generous to think I have ten years work in me. Van Gogh said he painted a painting per day. But I can't just paint. Even the idea of it; I'd prefer to live in darkness like a Gollum or some other troglodyte. How do I know that I won't get sick half-way through and regret not having spent my time watching ... Cary Grant films, or something? Put that way ... but try it and I'll become grouchy and morose. Artists are always grouchy, its inevitable when nineteen-twentieths of your life is spent in failure. But can I do it, is the question. Five hours a day ... that's less than I spend at school doing school-work. I could allow myself a drink or two of wine while I do it. But I know how that would work out. A drink or two, then I'd decide I'm sleepy, go to bed, wake up dried out and exhausted and stick on the TV with processed dinner and get up again later after having fallen asleep again and go to bed. Or maybe that's just the children tiring me out, using up all my unconscious energy. But then why do I never take up a paintbrush even during the summer holidays? Well, that's not quite true. I like to dabble. But how many years is it since I finished anything? I can't remember. It might even have been last century. How come this century lasted only five minutes? I can't understand it. I can't understand anything. Maybe I could paint trains passing rapidly and invisibly through space. Turner painted those a hundred and fifty years ago. There is nothing left to paint. Maybe Turner thought that too. Not my problem, anway, I'll be dead. Not going to get much glory, really. So to what purpose, then? Well, perhaps it serves as much purpose as anything. After all, if I watch TV, if I chat with my friends, the same space is decorated, but with nothing, or at best with water that quickly evaporates. If I can leave a mark on a stone and someone adds another mark, that is as much as can be hoped for. Not hugely inspiring. Well. Thirty minutes seem to have passed in but the twinkling of an eye and I didn't even fall asleep. I suppose I will pick up that paintbrush. Perhaps I should not think of the inevitability of putting it down again. It is a question of when it goes down. Perhaps, for as long as it is in my diminishing power, I should delay that moment.

```
INT. MOBILE CLASSROOM - DAY

All the tables and chairs have been
pushed back, and we are watching children
doing drama.

                    DIRECTOR
          What are they doing?

                    DAPHNE DONAGHY
          A re-enactment.
```

DIRECTOR
Of what?

DAPHNE DONAGHY
The making of the mine. The parents, most of them, seem happy enough for us to try it out.

DIRECTOR
You had to get permission?

DAPHNE DONAGHY
Of course. You can't do recreative therapy the same as you bake chocolate bread. There are forms to be filled in.

DIRECTOR
I had to fill in a few myself. There's three kids I have to keep making sure are out of shot.

DAPHNE DONAGHY
All the same, remarkable that most agreed to it.

DIRECTOR
I also told the parents that it would be therapeutic.

DAPHNE DONAGHY
They're a resilient bunch. Most are fine. No, that's not true. Many are traumatised in some way. But no overt signs of PTSD and I've been watching. So far so good. Just normal anxiety and nerves that we've got to work through.

DIRECTOR
Any PTSD yourself?

DAPHNE DONAGHY
Apart from the general feeling of dissoluteness and terror of my life going down the drain? I gave you my journal. My general mood has not changed compared to before.

DIRECTOR
Yes, thanks for sharing something so intimate. I'm still finding it difficult to understand your openness.

DAPHNE DONAGHY
It's simply that - what am I talking about? It's

not simple at all. It has to do with the empty state of my being and the need to do anything quickly rather than face the fate I was spelling out in that particular entry.

DIRECTOR
You mean, that awful fate of sitting in front of a nice toasty fire sipping wine and watching TV?

DAPHNE DONAGHY
You make it sound idyllic but it fills me with terror.

DIRECTOR
I totally understand. Well, that's a lie. Let me say, I have a glimmer of understanding. I'm the opposite at the moment and thinking of giving up documentary making altogether.

DAPHNE DONAGHY
You have a small child, if I recall?

DIRECTOR
Two years old.

DAPHNE DONAGHY
Life does tend to get in the way of ambition.

DIRECTOR
I'd always hoped my artistic stuff might supplement my life.

DAPHNE DONAGHY
That's more or less where I was forty years ago. It doesn't really matter anyway as long as you enjoy your life. But I think some people, and you're probably one of them, can't, so the next best thing is to do a bit of art in consolation.

DIRECTOR
That's it. You've summed up my entire being.

DAPHNE DONAGHY
Do you want to watch these children doing their re-enactment?

DIRECTOR
Yes. Let's film some of this, we can chat more later.

SEB DOUGLAS
I said get back down that mine wretch!
(cracks a whip)

GARRET TRAINER
(Cowers)
Yes Master

RUTH DUFFY
You smelly landowner! Take this!
(throws dynamite in his face)

SEB DOUGLAS
Miss! She's not meant to do that!

DAPHNE DONAGHY
(Sighs)
That's right. And we've spoken as well about the whip. They didn't use whips.

RUTH DUFFY
Then how did they make them go down the pit?

DAPHNE DONAGHY
We've spoken about that too. Does anyone remember?

(blank expressions, then:)

ORLAGH KEEGAN
(raises hand)
Miss.

DAPHNE DONAGHY
Orlagh.

ORLAGH KEEGAN
They didn't need whips because they had all the money.

DAPHNE DONAGHY
(Pause)
Yes. That's a good way of putting it. People need money to live, so they went down the mines to work. I think that's more or less the same reason anyone works.

RUTH DUFFY
But it was dangerous!
(Accidently shoves Seb Douglas)

SEB DOUGLAS
Ouch!

DAPHNE DONAGHY
Seb, Ruth, stop. Yes, it was dangerous. Now, you two, opposite sides of

the room, Ruth there, you there. But for the time maybe not so dangerous. Can anyone remember how many people died?

(Orlagh Keegan raises hand)

DAPHNE DONAGHY
Anyone?
(Waits)
Yes, good: Orlagh?

ORLAGH KEEGAN
There was a man who fell when they were digging.

RUTH DUFFY
I remember! He was in the can on his way down but then he got crushed against the side.

DAPHNE DONAGHY
(Aside to Director)
My goodness she can be articulate when it comes to death and destruction.
(To Ruth)
That's right, Ruth. And Orlagh. So what else can we remember? Were there any other injuries?

SEB DOUGLAS
(raises hand)
Miss.

DAPHNE DONAGHY
Yes Seb.

SEB DOUGLAS
The man who got his hand stuck.

RUTH DUFFY
(Raises hand excitedly and speaks before being asked)
Yes Miss! He was turned into spaghetti by the winch that raises the can up and down. Trapped his hand and it tore it off at the shoulder, and he always had to walk like this after.
(Mimics a hunchback after hoisting her arm out of her sleeve, which hangs loose)

DAPHNE DONAGHY
That is correct, except that he was not entirely turned into spaghetti, since he survived.
(Aside to Director)
And she's the one who looked into the pit. It

seems to have traumatised her not one bit. The reverse in fact.
(To class again)
So you'll notice: one death, one injury. If it happened today the mine might be closed. But back in those days just one death wasn't bad; it was quite good. Can anyone remember the big word we learned last time? About numbers, like numbers of deaths and injuries in different mines in Great Britain and Ireland as it was at the time?

          ORLAGH KEEGAN
(raises hand)
Miss.

          DAPHNE DONAGHY
Please go ahead Orlagh.

          ORLAGH KEEGAN
Miss, statistics

          DAPHNE DONAGHY
(Aside to Director)
So smart and bright that one. Daughter of my best friend Angela whom you've met. But there is something about her

brightness that fills me with dread. I've chatted to Angela about it. I told her that this child is destined for a high-flying career in the city, overcoming all obstacles. Angela beams with pride when I say that. I tell her I wouldn't wish that future on anyone. But I can see that the class want my attention again.
(to class)
Statistics. And if we compare the Carrickfergus mines of the time to those of, say, Cheshire, what do we find?

  ORLAGH KEEGAN
(raises hand)
Miss

  DAPHNE DONAGHY
I'm going to see if anyone else can answer this time. Fiona, for instance.

  FIONA MCALEESE
Miss … lower … mortality.

  DAPHNE DONAGHY
(Aside to Director)

Lower mortality! My goodness. You see, this is the problem with bright girls like Orlagh. They blind one to the hidden intelligences in the room. Fiona is quiet. As quiet as those proverbial mice whom, I must say, I suspect are living in the wainscoting of this mobile. Fiona comes from a highly religious family. The type of Catholicism that is sincere if you know what I mean. There's a depth to that kind of belief that I can never approach. I wonder what she made of it all? You might interview her.

          DIRECTOR
I've tried. Nothing.

        DAPHNE DONAGHY
I must get back to the class.
(To class)
Excellent Fiona.
(To Director)
I must tone it down. I think she reacts badly to praise.
(To class)

What does mortality mean?

(Orlagh raises hand)

        DAPHNE DONAGHY
I see you Orlagh, but I'd like again to give the others a chance. But please do keep raising your hand if you know, I'll ask you next. What about you, Bronagh?

        BRONAGH WARD
No Miss.

        DAPHNE DONAGHY
Garret?

(Garret shakes head)

        DAPHNE DONAGHY
Trevor?

(Trevor shakes head)

        DAPHNE DONAGHY
Orlagh?

        ORLAGH KEEGAN
It means the amount of people dead Miss Donaghy.

        DAPHNE DONAGHY
Absolutely correct. It means the number of

people killed in mining accidents, in this case. And you may remember it was lower in the Carrickfergus mines than any in Cheshire. Much lower. Although we don't have data for our particular mine. Who owned our mine?

RUTH DUFFY
Miss, no-one knows.

DAPHNE DONAGHY
Ruth, please raise your hand. But that's essentially correct. Except, is it true that no-one knows, or that we don't know?

RUTH DUFFY
Miss – sorry.
(raises hand)

DAPHNE DONAGHY
Yes Ruth.
(To Director)
This is too military. I'm going to relax this hand up stuff.
(To Ruth)
Go ahead.

RUTH DUFFY
Miss, I mean we don't know. But does someone know?

DAPHNE DONAGHY
We don't know if someone knows. All we know is that I went to the public records office, PRONI, and couldn't find anything. But I did find information on the mines owned by – who?

ORLAGH KEEGAN
(raises hand)
Miss.

DAPHNE DONAGHY
Yes Orlagh. And from now on no more raised hands, I'll point at people and if that person can't say then anyone can shout it out. Go on, Orlagh.

ORLAGH KEEGAN
Miss, it was the Markwiss … the Mr Qwuss … The …

DAPHNE DONAGHY
Close. Anyone?

BRONAGH WARD
The Marky!

DAPHNE DONAGHY
That's right. The Marquis of who? Jenny.

JENNY BURNS
Um ...

DAPHNE DONAGHY
Anyone.

SEB DOUGLAS
The Marky of Downsheer!

RUTH DUFFY
(With a scowl at Seb from across the room)
That's what I was about to say. Miss, he stole the words from my brain.

DAPHNE DONAGHY
Ruth, if he could do that from yours he could just as easily do it from mine. But I observe that Seb does not routinely finish my sentences for me.

DOWN THE MINE (PART III)

Elbert was not feeling well that morning.

'What's the matter with you?' asked Elbert's Mammy. 'You got the lurgy? A lurgy's no reason to be stayin in yer bed.'

'It's more than the lurgy, ma. It's like when Da hit me over the head that time. I keep seein these lights go on and off again.'

His ma tutted and felt his head. She withdrew her hand.

'Yer burnin like a christmas candle,' she said. 'What have ye been at?'

Elbert had a sense that last Saturday night might have something to do with it but last thing in the world he wanted was for his mother to know.

'Aye, I think it might have been the bad air of the mine,' Elbert said feebly.

Elbert's Ma looked at him long and hard. She left without saying anything, going downstairs. He heard her send his younger brother to the mine on a message.

McKnicken listened to this younger brother of Elbert with mounting impatience. 'Won't come, or can't come? I hire a man for a job and this is what I get. You got mining experience? What age are ye? We need an extra hand lifting them there buckets. You go down and hoist them to the line. There'll be a coin in it and a bowl of stew. And as for who'll go down–I'll go down meself. I know how to light as well as any man. I taught em after all. Now scamp away off to that fella over there, he'll tell you what needs doing.'

The young lad needed no further encouragement: he rushed over to the long shed. That's how McKnicken liked them, full of beans, not bonelazy like the Elberts and the Thomass became once they passed into their twenties. As if the mounding of rubble and blasting of rock no longer held enough spark for em. More concerned with chasin women. But then he supposed he'd not been much different when the money'd first entered his pocket. You never knew what to do with it at first not having had a mere penny's-worth before.

'Hoist me down lads,' said McKnicken, after rolling up his sleeves. He kept on his waistcoat.

The little metal tube slowly sank down into the depths of the shaft. Reaching the bottom, so gently that for a moment he thought they'd stopped winching halfway and he was suspended still in the air, McKnicken stepped out.

'Ah!' he said, beating his chest, breathing deep the close air. 'Smell of sulphur and dust. Get the dust deep in you, Henry McKnicken. Get it in yer lungs. Clean em out. No breath better than a gulp of good dusty mine air. Thomas. I see your light over yonder. Come here and we'll gather the tools.'

He remembered to pull the bell cord. 'Send down the packages boys,' he shouted up, even though he knew nothing useful would remain of his phrase by the time it bounced up to the surface.

He paused for a moment, looking up that tall tower at the little pinprick of sunlight above. So quiet down here. Peaceful, compared to the frenzy of the upabove world.

Thomas stood beside him. 'Where's Elbert?'

'He's off sick. I'm with ye the day Thomas. I'll show you how to carve out near double the weight ye's got out the day before!'

McKnicken's hearty laugh bounced off the walls of the crypt-like space.

'Christ in heaven!' said McKnicken, in response to Thomas's swing. 'What are ye puttin' the hole in there for? I told ye: like a honeycomb. You not seen a bee? That's nature's way. Ye've got to follow the masters. Right up there. Regular.'

Thomas spat on the ground. He pulled the pick back up. He brought the pick down hard on the rockface.

'That'll do?' he said, to McKnicken.

McKnicken ignored Thomas' tone. He raised the lantern and looked.

'Aye, it'll do. Fill it with 'nite and I'll gather em cables over.'

While Thomas filled the holes with dynamite, Henry took the lantern to locate a roll of wire. He circled it round his shoulder.

Returning, he looked with dissatisfaction at Thomas's packing of the holes. 'Naw, no like that. Look.'

Henry took Thomas' pick-axe, raised it above his head. Just as Henry swung he realised how stupid his act was. The pick connected. The hole exploded.

RUTH DUFFY'S DIARY

Today I went into Egypt. First we went back to the old school. There was a big pit in the ground. We went into it. It was me and Ali. We went into it and it was Quiet dark but we saw anyway because we Eat carrotes. Then we saw there was a big miner down ther with a beard that was actually a moustache. We said 'hey mr miner! and he looked shocked to see us down there! He was scared of us not us of him! So we went down to him. He was down ~~acrac crank~~ cranik shaft. And only had one arm. I said to him Which way to Egypt. He pointed and he went down this other passageway. I asked Ali if we should follow him or go to egypt. Ali didn't know sowe Talked about it for awhile and then decided that maybe we'd follow that man. It was on for miles and miles and twice I got lost and couldn't find Ali anymore. 'Hlep ali!' I shouted and she could here me because I heared her shout back. She was shouting 'help the octopus got me!' so I went and got a sharp stick that was There from the old mining Days and told Ali Keep shouting at me and I'll find you and the cotopus and then If ound the octopus and killed it. There was some Treauser there a magic ring which I put on. 'Help I'm being sucked away!' Luckily I could grab onto Ali's hand and she got sucked away into a nother big area. It was Egypt. It was like a Pyramid. We'd finally found it and were rich. 'Look at all this' and ti was like a miners best dream beacuse their was jules and lots of gold. Of course I was born on the sun so dont' need gold but it was good for christmas. Imagine Mum when she saw that! I put too golds in my pocket and some preciose rings. Then ali asked: how do we get home again? And I said 'easy' and there was another ring and "woosh!' I ws back in time again before we went back and so was Ali.

Director's notes
I went to see my mentor, Mike. He was more worried looking than he normally is. Kept on glancing right and left, kept on taking hurried sips from his cocktail. 'Things are tight at the moment,' he kept saying. 'Yes, but how can I get some money?' I asked. I needed Mike to tell me how to get the money. 'Current environment is putting a real squeeze on freelance work like this at the moment. Tell me again about your project?' And the more I told him about my project the less attention he gave to what I was telling him. He was practically having a different conversation with the guy next door before I'd finished. Then he was out hailing a taxi saying he'd get in touch very soon.

I am uncertain whether this project is going to get further funding.

INT. WALL - DAY

Clock on wall now reads twenty-five past three. A shock and it falls precipitously. Cut to a broken clock lying smashed in a load of glass down below.

THE COLLAPSE CONTINUES

Finbar Adams runs back in awkwardly negotiating the doorway with a huge ladder in hand. He is in the room when the largest shock yet throws him to the floor where he flies down to the far end where the blackboard is. He hits it. The sledge hammer is sliding towards him. He realises it is heading directly for his face. At the last possible second he gets off his back and leaps out of the way as the ten pound head smashes into the wall just below the blackboard pulverising the brickwork and raising a cloud of dust.

'Could ey bin me fuckin head!' he mutters, heart pounding.

He gets up, dusting himself off.

'Dust all over me,' he says.

He looks at the sledge hammer, wanting to get going with some sledging, but suppressing the urge, knowing that sledging in the wrong place could make the difference between life and death for some wain or even himself. He has to pick his spot. He casts a skeptical eye on the whole frame of the room, considering what it might look like if he bashed this bit here or that bit there. Finally he settles on a point that seems best. It's a bit over near the window. He thinks that after he's cut the offending girder truss above that's the pivot point everything is going to turn on. He looks into himself and asks how he knows this but all he can tell himself is there isn't time to think. He says to himself he can think about it afterwards as much as he wants over a rollie and a cuppa tea.

So up the ladder he scurried. There was dust up here eons old and pencils kids had been throwing up despite the fact they could blind someone, and also a rubber band tied in two. He looked down even though it always gave the heebies to be up a ladder and look down. It gave him the heebies this time and he regretted it. Still, time to be sawing before the next one came because he'd be thrown off his ladder then no two ways about it. From this height it wouldn't just be a tiny bit of a sore ankle or a bit of a bruise on the head, it'd be a twisted something if not something broke and that's assuming nothing came crashing down on top of him. He sawed with fury. There was a cracking sound and he hurried down the ladder before the whole roof came down on him.

'That's a point,' he said to himself, picking up the sledge and going to wall. He busted it into the wall once or twice then had a quick look at the roof where he'd sawn the girder and then the door where the P3s had exited into the P4 classroom. He needed to be through that door in instants if not quicker at the moment this whole thing folded in. But he had to keep whacking away at this wall until it folded in like to make sure it folded in the way he wanted it to which was a way of folding that didn't do damage to the classroom the wains and the teachers were in. Then there might be a chance of gettin everyone out but that was too far ahead to be thinking of so he put his shoulder to it got a clear hole in the wall and bits of glass and dust all around him and he had a brief laugh thinking how all the banging and wood and splinters were probably sounding to the hosts back there in the other classroom and them thinking it was probably madness. It was madness. He put his energies now into sledging the floor in a line from the hole in the wall over under the girder truss and towards the other side of the wall and now it felt as if the floor was leaning dangerously in the blackboard direction so he started to feel the pit falling in his stomach something telling him to get to fuck get to fuck out of here and into the other classroom but fought against it because the wains'd get squashed and he with them if he didn'a do it right so he kept at it bashing and sledging the unfortunate floor until he reached the other wall where sweating profusely he paused for a wee minute wipe his face and look up and look over and consider what he'd done and what he might need to do.

INT. MOBILE CLASSROOM - DAY

Finbar Adams sitting on kid's chair at a kid's desk.

>   DIRECTOR
> That sounds terrifying.

>   FINBAR ADAMS
> Aye.

THE COLLAPSE CONTINUES

Meanwhile inside the classroom Miss Donaghy was considering their exit strategy.

If we go out those windows the children might get cut. Half the windows are shattered. If we go out the door but the roof collapses then all the children die. How long would it take them to run out? And when we're out, how do they climb that sheer slope?

Finbar had several ladders. She would need to talk to Finbar, get him to help them out. He would be able to knock a window through and if they passed the children over one at a time they might be able to transport them all outside without any serious gashes or injuries.

'I need to talk to Finbar,' Miss Donaghy told Miss McTaggart.

Miss McTaggart acknowledged this and led the class in animal noise identification.

Miss Donaghy went through the storeroom and stood in the P3 doorway. Finbar was smashing and hammering everything in sight in an apparent frenzy of destruction.

'Finbar!' she shouted angrily. 'What are you doing?'

Finbar straightened up like a child caught in some bad act.

'Oh, Miss, just, trying to get the classroom to collapse right way.'

'Well stop it and come in and help me knock through a window. We'll need that ladder as well.'

Finbar shook his head, as if it cost him dearly to refuse.

'Naw, miss, but if I don't keep collapsing at this classroom thing'll coup wrong and drag the rest of us away wi' it. So if you dont mind I'm gonna keep on bein here.'

Miss Donaghy strode over to the big ladder.

'I'm taking this,' she said.

'Nay Miss, no yet! Dinnae ye see the strain on these walls!'

Miss Donaghy glanced at the walls and could see nothing. But Finbar seemed convinced that the big one was about to come at any moment and indeed had set about his labour again, banging and hurling the sledgehammer about. Miss Donaghy dragged the tall wooden ladder awkwardly behind her. It wouldn't fit. It was too long and the doors were at too-tight angles. There was a tremor. She grabbed both sides of the doorframe in terror.

She exhaled, fearing the worst was yet to come.

Finbar had paused momentarily in his hammering but now went at it with renewed vigour. She had no idea what he was doing but now she felt that some dreadful final lurch was imminent. She returned to the Primary Four classroom.

'Children,' she shouted, above the cacophony of farmyard noises. 'Soon there will be a big huge lurch – what does lurch mean? Lurch means a big fall. It'll feel bad but we'll be ok.' She didn't believe it herself. It didn't matter if she believed it. 'And we'll be fine. Hold on tight to the desk. And I want everyone to close their eyes and think about Christmas. Snow falling down, and your favourite toys, and the lovely roast dinner and chocolate log. After the next big fall we're going to get out to safety and there will warm blankets and big hugs. From your Mummies and Daddies.'

```
INT. DUFFY LIVINGROOM - DAY

Elizabeth and Padraig Duffy sitting
together on the sofa.

                DIRECTOR
        And you were in time to
        see it?

                ELIZABETH DUFFY
        I can't close my eyes at
        night without seeing it.
```

                    DIRECTOR
            Tell me what you saw.

                THE COLLAPSE CONTINUES
Elizabeth Duffy saw a crater with the lower half of the school in it. About two metres below ground level and shifting awkwardly to one side as if some giant unseen hand were dragging it under. She turned to Padraig. He looked as if he was about to fall headfirst into it. She took his hand, steadying them both. Looking back at the school she saw it go crump and slip an extra inch into the ground.

'Christ!' said Padraig. 'Ruth's in there!'

They ran round the side of the school to look through the P4 window. The sun was reflecting off the glass so they couldn't see inside.

'We've got to go down,' said Padraig, ready to leap in the hole.

'How are you going to get back out? Don't we need help?' Elizabeth asked, putting a restraining hand on his arm. Then she thought to herself that this was just fear and that he was right and they both had to get down.

'Ok,' she said. 'Well then let me give you a hand. And then I'm coming down too.'

'I'll slide down this raggedy bit here, and then you leap down a few stones and we'll get down.'

Elizabeth frowned. 'Kids won't be able to get back up. We need a ladder or something.'

'We'll lift a bit of a door. There'll be something. Can't stand here!'

'Well ... then let's go down. Let's try it.'

They skidded down the slope together. It was almost but not entirely vertical. The ground at the base was sodden with water.

'Ah, bloody hell ... what's this? The bloody pipes have burst.'

Of course the pipes had burst, thought Elizabeth. Would there be water inside? She thought of children in there drowning in rising brackish water and hurried, squelching, through the mud to the windows. The sun was still bouncing off them, but she thought she could discern a shape there. Something waving. Waving at her? Or telling her...?

She heard Daphne Donaghy's command to get out of the way, and did so, and a chair smashed through the window.

'Help me get the glass out of the way,' said Miss Donaghy. 'Finbar was meant to but all I can get out of him is talk about a stream. He's lost it.'

Finbar, meanwhile, was talking to himself about a stream of water that was flowing across the P4 classroom into the P3 classroom and away. It was the away bit that had him worried. It didn't fit with his image. If he'd been hammering and sledging over there, what the hell was that water doing over there, trickling down into – what? It should be mounting up. There should be a big wall of gravel or whatever. That's why he'd been blasting at the sous-structure in the middle so that it'd fold up like a deck of cards in that direction ...

Finbar stepped back to get a better look at the blackboard wall in the P3 classroom when that entire wall fell backwards away from him, falling down into nothing, entirely disappearing from view and revealing an apparently bottomless pit on the other side.

'Oh shit,' he said, advancing towards it in the way you advance towards the edge of a cliff knowing there is absolutely nothing to be gained from doing so but unable to resist the view.

He could confirm that the pit was indeed bottomless. The masonry and the blackboard had wedged about three metres down a hole that was about three metres in diameter. He could see nothing beyond it: blackness. He felt giddy, thinking he might coup into it. He felt about for something to steady himself but there was nothing there. He turned round, slipping on the wet floor, managing to fall flat on the ground rather than tipping backwards into the pit.

'Crump' went the whole lower half of the school, and sunk precipitously a few more feet downwards like stepping in deep snow.

Finbar scrabbled along the floor which had developed an even more pronounced tilt, and then the roof fell on top of him, god knows what had kept it up so long given all the sawing and bashing he'd been doing and the whole back wall missing now it folding over him bashing him with wood and tiles and fucking masonry. He covered his head wishing he'd brought a hardhat. He went deaf in one ear the sound was so horrendous. Dust and debris filled the air so that he choked and coughed. But somehow he was still alive. It was only then he realised something must have hit him, without him feeling it, because his back was in enormous pain. He howled like an animal.

'Got to get the fuck out of here,' he shouted, and started crawling towards the P4 door. It was obviously no-go, there: the fallen roof blocked the way. He got up on his hands and knees and then onto his feet. He looked round at the other end of the classroom, the end that had fallen into that bottomless pit that had opened up under the school.

'Bloody hell,' he said, retreating from what looked to be the damn thing opening up under his feet. It was just the optics, the way the floor slanted, but unnerving, easily the most unnerving thing he'd experienced in many a long while of unnerving horrible things. He walked backwards gingerly as if afraid his slightest wrong movement might send the entire delicate structure of the school further into the hole even though it couldn't possibly all fit. But that wasn't what the school was falling into anyway, there was some other space down there, else this big damned crater wouldn't have opened up all around. Why they build a school on top of a big empty space, were they stupid? He retreated another step and slipped again on the wet ground, the stream heading steadily now and dropping into the hole like a waterfall.

Got to get out a window or sommut, he thought, as clear as day, and he looked right to consider his options. That wall was still standing, somehow, and the windows pretty smashed up and dangerous looking. Less dangerous than that pit though. Yes. Get through one of those, he thought.

He got up again, pain in his back competing with his ankle. Ouch ouch ouch, bloody sore, he thought. Bloody bloody sore. He got up as far as the cupboards and then hoisted himself up. Wished he had his toolkit, maybe take the edge off these windows before rolling over and out of them. Aye. His goddam toolkit he'd spent years putting together, lost, down this stupid hole. Better get it. Then he remembered the big wooden ladder he'd been using to get at the girder truss. Needed that more. Where was it? Lying there, didn't look broke, under – yes – the big fecking girder truss itself. Well there was no option, he needed to get it.

```
INT. BOILER ROOM - DAY

Finbar Adams is polishing a brass poker.
As usual the boiler room is gloomy.
Finbar himself is full of cheer.
```

FINBAR ADAMS
Ho-hum. Hum a deedle dee.

DIRECTOR
How have you been feeling, lately?

FINBAR ADAMS
Eh? Feeling? I've been feeling … it's gettin into summer. Be all right, gettin a wee summer break. Much as I like the wains an all.

DIRECTOR
I mean, have you had nightmares? Or counseling? Did the authorities offer you any counseling?

FINBAR ADAMS
Naw.

DIRECTOR
Did you want any?

FINBAR ADAMS
Counseling? Naw. Naw.

DIRECTOR
(aside to herself)
He said it twice.
(To Finbar)
Sure?

                    FINBAR ADAMS
          Aye.

INT. MOBILE CLASSROOM - DAY

Director sits on a schoolchild's chair. She looks distracted. Daphne Donaghy comes into frame.

                    DAPHNE DONAGHY
          How do.

                    DIRECTOR
          Not terrifically well.

                    DAPHNE DONAGHY
          I'm sorry to hear that.
          What's the matter?

                    DIRECTOR
          They aren't going to fund
          me.

                    DAPHNE DONAGHY
          Oh. You mean, the people
          you were applying to fund
          the rest of this
          documentary.

                    DIRECTOR
          Funny thing is, I thought
          I wouldn't care.

> DAPHNE DONAGHY
> Do you?
>
> DIRECTOR
> Yes.
>
> DAPHNE DONAGHY
> What will you do?
>
> DIRECTOR
> Well ... not documentary making, anyway.
>
> DAPHNE DONAGHY
> Don't give up just because of one rejection.
>
> DIRECTOR
> One? I wish it was only one.

Director's notes

It certainly was not only one. It's part of the business. You keep throwing proposals out there and hope one sticks. I blamed my early success. That'd encouraged me, years back, to have a go of it. But this rejection felt final. It was as if I'd chased my monster as far as I could, to the ends of the Earth. Bitterness ... I could be bitter, but why? That's it. I have to earn money doing something else. Civil servant probably. At the weekends do singer-songwriter gigs. Save up for a mortgage.

Water fills the hole. You forget about it. No sign of the trauma beneath the surface.

INT. DUFFY LIVINGROOM - DAY

Elizabeth and Padraig as before

> ELIZABETH DUFFY
> When we saw that wall of the P3 classroom going over, I thought I was going to have a heart attack.

> PADRAIG DUFFY
> I definitely did have a heart attack. Like someone had put their hand round my heart and squeezed it.

> ELIZABETH DUFFY
> You did look rather gray, come to think of it.

> PADRAIG DUFFY
> There was dust too. Anyway. That mad bastard the Janitor appears at the bloody window with a ladder.

> ELIZABETH DUFFY
> That was a few minutes later.

> PADRAIG DUFFY
> No, I think it took us time to get up.

ELIZABETH DUFFY
It happened fast. We saw the ladder first, poking out, and ran down to get it.

PADRAIG DUFFY
Slipped and slid. Thing was like some WWI trench or something. Like, we just needed rats and chlorine.

ELIZABETH DUFFY
So under the cover of machine gun fire –

PADRAIG DUFFY
Naw, let's not joke.

ELIZABETH DUFFY
I find it helpful to joke.

PADRAIG DUFFY
Well then go ahead.

ELIZABETH DUFFY
We grabbed hold of that ladder. But Finbar wouldn't let go of it, as if it was his lifeline too. I think he only had a vague grasp of what was going on at this point.

In fact we didn't know either at this point who was holding the ladder or what, because everything looked the same kind of dry-mud dust-brown to me.

PADRAIG DUFFY
And me.

ELIZABETH DUFFY
You pulled at the ladder and Finbar fell over.

PADRAIG DUFFY
I wouldn't have done it if I'd known he was two foot from a hole of death.

ELIZABETH DUFFY
Finbar told us afterwards that he nearly jumped into the hole just out of spite because he was so fed up with everything going wrong for him.

PADRAIG DUFFY
He had a broke ankle. They found that out later. Not just twisted. I don't know how he got around on it.

ELIZABETH DUFFY
Sometimes you don't feel pain under these situations. I remember once I was out dancing on a bad ankle and it was only when I got home I realised that it was swollen up so that I couldn't take off my shoe.

PADRAIG DUFFY
Luckily he didn't fall in the hole. He just landed beside it. We could hear him cursing and wailing.

ELIZABETH DUFFY
I think we took the ladder out and over to the wall, the big wall of mud and boulders and stuff, the crater wall.

PADRAIG DUFFY
I can't remember that bit, actually. I can't remember going into the classroom or how I did it. Maybe you put the ladder over and I climbed into the classroom through the window. I had cuts in my hands after but don't know if it was

from that or the P4 window.

ELIZABETH DUFFY

Or both. I think we both took the ladder over and then you went into the classroom, but you seemed to just jump straight through it without touching anything.

PADRAIG DUFFY

I thought there were children in there, the wee P3s, just like Ruth had been in there the year before. The roof fallen in … I didn't want to think about that. Just went in, and maybe I was asking Finbar about it as I went in, because he said that all the children were in the other room, P4, that it was just him here. I almost left him to go and see those kids but helped him up anyway.

ELIZABETH DUFFY

I'd already abandoned the pair of them. I think normally I wouldn't have been able to carry a ladder like that – it was about three metres long, very heavy! I don't remember how I did it but I brought it all the way to that bit of the crater we'd climbed down and then returned to the P4 classroom window where the kids were climbing out onto the ground.

PADRAIG DUFFY
I saw that bloody hole in the ground. The whole back wall of the school had fallen into it. It was just gone. Finbar said the blackboard got lodged but there was nothing there just this stream from the broken pipes falling down and down and disappearing like some fucking … I don't know. Hell.

DIRECTOR
You thought the pit of Hell had opened up beneath you?

PADRAIG DUFFY
There was no fire down there but it was definitely a bad-looking

deep hole in the ground. And it was ringed by all these broken planks of wood, all rotten like. That's not how I see the mouth of Hell.

          DIRECTOR
Planks of wood. Sticking out like teeth?

          PADRAIG DUFFY
I suppose so.

          DIRECTOR
And Elizabeth … what then? Did you see Ruth?

          ELIZABETH DUFFY
No. She didn't come out. It was P3s first, they decided younger ones got the first go out.

          DIRECTOR
And you were helping them out?

          ELIZABETH DUFFY
I'd take them one by one, pass them onto the ground.

> DIRECTOR
> And you, Padraig, were in the P3 classroom at this point?

> PADRAIG DUFFY
> That's right. I was helping Finbar up. We got over to the window when there was another big jolt and everything went sliding to fuck into that big pit.

THE COLLAPSE CONTINUES

'Ah fuck, ah fuck,' cried Finbar, falling onto his serially-abused ankle, and everything started sliding southwards into the maw of the pit.

'Shite,' said Padraig, who had been helping Finbar over to the window, thinking they might climb out of it, when he and Finbar had been thrown to the ground again. 'We're going to go under ...'

Padraig didn't want to go under, so he grabbed hold of a passing table. Problem was this passing table was passing towards the hole at the other side of the classroom, and was likely to vanish down it. He let go and tried to scrabble to his feet, but the water splashing everywhere combined with the non-grip linoleum floor meant rising was a near impossibility. He half-rolled, half-scurried towards the cupboards at the side of the room. This meant working with the downwards direction of the classroom and going diagonal where possible. He managed to grab a cupboard handle but that was uncomfortably close to the enormous hole in the ground.

Finbar had not been so fortunate. He had skidded and fallen almost to the very edge of the pit, and had nothing obvious to hold on to.

INT. BOILER ROOM - DAY

Finbar Adams drinking from a Thermos flask.

>   FINBAR ADAMS
> I thought I was done for at that point. Soaked through from splashing in the water, and couldna bear hold of anything. There was a bit of a jaggedy slope at the edge of the hole, so I could rest my feet on that, but the room was like at 30° angle or something at that point, and all this shite coming towards me in crissy-cross skids, so I knew I couldna really hold on long. I'd get whacked by someut sooner or later. Probly sooner.
>
>   DIRECTOR
> Lucky Padraig was there.
>
>   FINBAR ADAMS
> Aye but at this point he cudna do anything for me,

he was hanging on this cupboard door which was hangin loose anyway, it's not meanta take a big weight like that lug Padraig. Surprised it didne break outright.

DIRECTOR
So you were just both hanging in there, hoping you wouldn't get whacked or otherwise fall in.

FINBAR ADAMS
That's right. And of all the bloody things, what suddenly appears up at the top end, as if we dinnae have enough to contend with then already?

DIRECTOR
What?

FINBAR ADAMS
The wain.

THE COLLAPSE CONTINUES
Ruth Duffy had a feeling she heard something familiar beneath the shouts and screams in her own classroom and the sounds of crashing and breaking and collapsing going on in the P3 classroom and concluded that

somehow her father was in there. She didn't know this directly, on a conscious level, but had an image of him vaguely in her head so decided to go have a look. Miss Donaghy and Miss McTaggart were otherwise distracted with mobilising the P3s for a swift exit so Ruth crawled between the tables on the floor. She reached the P4 door to the inter-classroom store when the big jolt came and she fell in to it, ended up hitting the wall on the opposite side as a whole pile of books did the same. She was very confused. The place didn't look like she remembered. Also there was a strange slope to the ground. She felt fine, not hurt, so got up and peeked out the P3 door. The P3 classroom was a devastated mess. The roof was gone; it had fallen onto the ground; and there was a big rip in the ground, as if some giant had broken the classroom over his knee. There were big clouds of dust rising up all over the place, and water flooding all over the ground, and she could barely see to the bottom, but she could hear people shouting and one of them was her Daddy, saying things in a bad language she had not thought he knew. She shouted his name: 'Daddy!' And she shouted it several times, but she thought her Daddy was saying too many bad things to hear her, and there was a big noise of tables rolling along the ground and a creaking sidewall about to fall over which meant there was nearly no chance he'd hear her if she kept going. But she did hear the Janitor shouting at her to stay put and he called her 'wain' as if he couldn't remember her name. The Janitor was like this. She advanced into the classroom despite the Janitor's orders to her but it was all slidey and she slipped on the wet surface and threw her hands out and managed to cling to a fallen lump of timber from the roof which was stuck in the ground. One of her shoes came off. She looked down the bumpy and all-over-the-place slope and wondered why the Janitor and her Daddy who she could see were just hanging on to things and didn't get up and get out.

Her Daddy saw her too, and looked very afraid and maybe angry so that she thought she should get back into the P4 classroom but at the same time she wanted to help her Daddy because he looked so afraid. So instead of getting out, getting out, as her Daddy kept saying and pointing away from himself she climbed over to the side of the room where the cupboards were and slid and half-walked, half-fell down towards him and when she reached him she said 'Daddy! I've come to get you.'

Her Daddy seemed momentarily speechless but then recovered and then said look Ruth we've got to climb all the way back up out of here and there's a big hole over there and I can't really see what's under my feet at the moment so I'm afraid to let go. Can you tell Daddy what's under his feet and if he's going to slide into a big hole if he lets go?

Ruth stood up and had a look and told her Daddy that he was frightened of nothing because the big hole was over there and if he let go he'd be on a bit of ground with grass and bricks on it.

Her Daddy let go of the cupboard door and closed his eyes and then with some relief on his face felt his feet touch solid ground so he got up and held on tight to the wall.

'Darling, the hole is a little bit closer to me than I would have liked ...'

'I know, Daddy, but you're all right, and you would've been scared to go if I'd told you.'

Daddy looked at the hole, which started about two foot away, and shuddered like they did in books. He didn't seem willing to let go of the wall. He kept looking at the hole and getting grey or white. Meantime the Janitor was shouting things and being angry. This distracted Daddy from the hole, and he decided that they needed something like a ladder for Finbar to lever himself onto because he wasn't going anywhere near that f*king hole. Ruth was shocked.

'Ruth, darling, come slowly down to Daddy and we're going out to Mummy who is just outside.'

Ruth looked at the big hole which, now she was being asked to go near it, looked very dark indeed, and she had that funny butterflies feeling you get when you are on a big ferris wheel or when you see those pictures of men eating sandwiches making the Empire State building or doing a tightrope walk. She shook her head.

'Ruth Duffy, you're going to have to come down here. You got me into this mess, now you come too. Just hold on to the sides and then slide down and you'll come right down beside my feet and then we'll walk easily round and up that hill there without looking back down and we'll go get the big ladder and get Finbar out of the big hole.'

'You'll no get that ladder over ye pillock!' shouted Finbar the Janitor and he said some other bad words too, much worse than pillock. He told Ruth's daddy that the f*cking ladder weighed a dead weight and would coup them all in the hole if they even tried to shimmy it over, and sure what was the counterweight going to be, Padraig F*cking Duffy that was as skinny as a malinky greyhound? No, Finbar was going to shimmy round except his ankle was bucked so he could only put weight on that other foot.

Ruth chose this moment to slide down the hill towards her Daddy, bumping into him when he didn't expect it. He suddenly grabbed her with both hands, tottered, and for a moment it was almost like they'd both fall over, and Ruth didn't like that, even though there was space enough that if they fell they wouldn't fall into the hole they'd fall beside it. But they didn't fall, they managed to stay upright. Finbar was still shouting and trying to put some weight on a foot where he was sort-of half-standing, half-lying down on the lip of the hole. He said he couldna think of a way to do it but to get that wain round the corner and he'd follow on somehow. Padraig said he'd take Ruth up but he'd be back soon as and he'd bring the ladder. Finbar cursed him out telling him not to get the f-ing ladder or he pelt himself straight into the hole hadn't he been listening to a bloody word? Padraig was already climbing up the slope, pushing Ruth ahead of him as he went, their hands getting covered with mud and the stones being sore on their palms but it wasn't a bad slope and they got up, seeing P3 kids lining up beside a ladder which had been placed up against a big wall of mud and boulders up into the playground above. Some of the children weren't wanting to go up, Ruth could see, it being scary, so Ruth's Mummy – Mummy! she shouted – she ran over to her. She was trying to tell someone that she needed to get out and start helping the kids up. Ruth couldn't see Miss Donaghy, she was round the corner. She hugged her Mummy round her legs. 'Ruth!' said Mummy with surprise and turned and saw Padraig coming over too. 'We've got to get Finbar out of there,' he said, pointing where they came. Mummy told him the children were going up the ladder but weren't going up and he had to carry them up. He seemed to forget Finbar and lifted a tiny P3 up into his arms and started climbing up with Mummy holding onto the ladder down below.

Director's notes
I went fishing in the local library, following up on a conversation with Daphne. She'd said something about still waters running deep. So, after fishing, I found a newspaper clipping with Finbar's name on it.

INT. MOBILE CLASSROOM - DAY

Director and Daphne Donaghy both in frame, sitting at a table eating packed lunches while kids play outside somewhere; occasional shouts are heard.

> DIRECTOR
> Is that Seb and Ruth playing together as if they were fast friends?

> DAPHNE DONAGHY
> (Laughs and nearly chokes on sandwich)
> My, how little you know of children. Of course they are fast friends. As the twin talents of the classroom they will love and hate each other for as long as they are both in this school.

> DIRECTOR
> (hesitates)
> I found this.

> DAPHNE DONAGHY
> (Takes piece of paper, unfolds it)
> I see. Good detective work.

> DIRECTOR
> I suppose so.

DAPHNE DONAGHY
(hands it back)
So what are you going to do?

DIRECTOR
I don't know.

DAPHNE DONAGHY
(after a pause)
You don't know? Doesn't a Director like you know what to do with a bit of paper like this?

DIRECTOR
Yeah. But am I a director?

DAPHNE DONAGHY
I always assumed that was the kind of thing you decided yourself.

DIRECTOR
No. Not something I can decide. I'm a bit confused about it.

DAPHNE DONAGHY
Well, as far as I'm concerned that's a normal state of being.

DIRECTOR
(looks at newspaper clipping)
Two men in a car. A crash. And because of concussion, it reports, the survivor can't remember what happened.

DAPHNE DONAGHY
He never speaks of it.

DIRECTOR
Obviously it would be a big reveal. Beneath those still waters, the trauma. It would save the film.

DAPHNE DONAGHY
He breaks down, you film it, everyone cries. Catharsis achieved.
(pause)
And yet here you are, waving that piece of paper in my face, rather than in his.

DIRECTOR
(shrugs)
What can you do?

THE COLLAPSE CONTINUED

Finbar was trying to see if he could just roll his way out, or crawl, to avoid putting weight on that dodge ankle. Must be real bad by now if he couldn't even use it in a life-death situation. He rested all his weight under one knee, holding onto a pipe sticking out under the schoolroom foundations. If the place gave another heave like earlier he'd be away down the tube and who knew how long it would take for him to bash into the bottom of that endless shaft. He pulled himself up a bit. Drudgery. Worse than drudgery even. The pipe was slippy with grease and water so he had to keep shifting his grip on it. At least the damned slope wasn't vertical here –

A little bit of ground gave way under his knee and he slipped down, desperately clawing at the greasy pipe, failing to secure a grip, and sliding down the slope. He grabbed the ground, dug his fingernails in, spread-eagled. It stopped his descent but now he had no means of actually getting back up. But staying here wasn't an option either. He wondered if that blackboard was still stuck down below, and if he'd land on it if he fell. He doubted it: all sorts of blocks of masonry had been tumbling down there and the blackboard wasn't tough enough to take that kind of beating forever. And maybe the bottomless hole wasn't bottomless after all and if he went he'd hit the bottom with maybe just a few broken legs. Aye, and then the rest of the school falling in after him. There was nought but bits of piping and shite cement holding this damn thing in place for a few minutes longer. But still he couldn't move. The pipe was well out of reach. What else was there? Over a bit, a lump of concrete sticking out. If he could get hold of that, great. But there was water flowing down between him and that and that would be slippy as fuck to try and get across. He'd be mental to try it. He suddenly felt thirsty looking at it and wondered what the fuck, was a drink of water really the best thing he could be having right now? He ignored it and wondered if he could wedge his good foot onto something, take the weight off his body. He was glad he was a bit pudgy round the middle, made a bit of a cushion for him to press on. If he was a scrawny fuck like Padraig Duffy he'd be away down the shaft by now. He wondered if the man was going to come back. The ladder was pointless unless they had it fixed to someut. But even a pole or something, but it'd need a load of nails on it or something so he could get a good grip because he wasn't going to trust to some slippy fucking pole. Slip off it and down into the pit. It didn't seem like anyone was going to come back anyway. He tried finding something to stand on and the first bit of ground his good foot touched broke off. Well fuck this thought Finbar.

Up on the surface other parents were beginning to congregate. They wore various expressions of helpless shock and inability to understand, but Elizabeth Duffy managed to shout them into some kind of assistance, stop them just gawking over the side, and start collecting the kids that Padraig was ushering up the big wooden ladder. P3s were going first and Elizabeth and Miss Donaghy were holding the ladder while Miss McTaggart kept tight control of the rabble of remaining children. All in a straight line, fingers on their lips, even under these conditions. She was a remarkable woman. Ruth was beside Elizabeth as if the presence of a parent down here trumped all other rules of school. She was tugging insistently on Elizabeth's jumper, telling her something unimportant about the Janitor, about him needing a ladder or somesuch, and Elizabeth trying to keep the ladder steady and her own nerves. She looked down. Ruth was crying, there were tears on her face. 'It'll be all right, Ruth,' she said, even though she didn't feel it.

'No, Mummy, Finbar the Janitor is still down there and he needed us to help him.'

'We need to get these children up, darling. I'm sure Finbar will take care of himself.'

'He won't Mummy, he's got a sore leg and he was about to fall into the big hole when we saw him!'

Something of the awfulness of this image roused Elizabeth away from the here and now and she realised that if Ruth was right there was something needed done about the Janitor. Miss Donaghy could probably hold the ladder just fine by herself. Although ... Miss Donaghy was someone you'd like in a situation like this. She mentioned to Miss Donaghy that according to her daughter the Janitor was in mortal peril.

'Right,' said Miss Donaghy. She signaled to a standing parent. 'Down this ladder and hold it. Padraig you keep ushering them up meanwhile.'

Without further explanation the two women, and Ruth, scrambled down the hill towards the suspended Finbar.

Finbar had his face in the dirt, exasperated and fatigued beyond remedy. His good foot and his bad foot alike hung helplessly over the void. No movements were possible in this context, as each was as likely to coup him as save him. Nevertheless he lifted his head for the tenth time, to see if a scan of that close horizon would reveal something it hadn't before, like maybe a piece of wire he could haul himself out on, or a magical rope, or just any fucking thing would be good. But there was naught but mud, and it was getting muddier too, which meant that the stream was sodding into it all and that wasn't good because it meant the whole thing Finbar was resting on would get heavier and more liquidy at the same time, a bad combination, bad if you wanted to stay exactly where you were without precipitating to your doom. He raised a meagre hand ahead of himself and the act caused him to slip an extra inch further down the slope. He kept his hand outstretched, unwilling to risk a return movement. Bloody thing was a hapless mess. Parts of his life flashed in front of his eyes: his boozing in the old days, his coming off the booze, his applying for the Janitor job and getting it. It had been a simple life. He couldn't think now whether he regretted any of it or was happy with any of it. For some reason he kept thinking of all those tools, lost. Presumably lost. Presumably his beloved boiler room was going to sink into the abyss like all the rest of this school and surrounds.

There came some sounds, he heard. Something or other, sounded like his name they were shouting. He wondered whether they could see him, and he tried to tell them to go away, that he was just fine where he was, but the voice wouldn't come out of him, it was too afraid to come out and give the ground even the smallest shake.

I'm bucked, he thought, *and so are they if they come any nearer.*

He didn't have a sense of who it was or where exactly they were, but he did know that unless they had some amazing rescue equipment, like maybe ropes all securely fastened with those clips and all, and hard hats, and picks, and unless they could slide down on that setup and grab him and then get hoisted up pretty fast that any attempt to come near him would see them all tip over the side and that was pointless. So he raised his voice a bit and told them to go away. There was a voice of a little girl then saying excitedly that that was Finbar. So maybe they couldn't see him. How far over the edge was he to fuck? He didn't want to look up or down or sideways any longer so didn't. He kept his face in the mud and his belly flat on the surface and his fingernails of both hands dug into whatever they could find.

'It's going to be hard to get him from there. Ground's all slippy and we've nothing to help him with.' That was P4 teacher, Miss Donaghy.

'Well, couldn't we ... isn't there a rope, or something we could wedge into the ground, that he could stand on, or ...'

'Not from this angle and I wouldn't like to move over that floor, if that's what you can call it. Ruth, stay by your Mama.'

'Stay by me darling.'

'I can see a bit of a ladder there!'

'It's all buried darling. And what would we do with it?'

'We need something he can hold on to. Something maybe like a big pole. These, look, we can go to the window and tear down a bit of the frame. There's a bit out already.'

Finbar heard, or imagined he heard, a bit of wood being ripped out of place, and a sigh.

'It's very short, isn't it? Ruth, keep hold of my hand, darling.'

'It's all we've got. Now. How good is it? If he holds on to that, is it secure? Are we going to be in a position to haul him up? I don't know about you, Elizabeth, but I am not in the habit of pulling lumps of men out of perilous pits relying on nothing but my own bodily strength.'

Finbar wondered whether to let go and stop them couping themselves in the pit but he couldn't will himself to do it. He wanted to live and not just fall down there in the hole. He wished he had a dozen rollies that he could smoke all at once right now. He felt about with his good foot. There had to be a kind of purchase. If he got his foot on someut and then they threw down that stick and he got hold of that with a hand, and if they didn't even coup in but somehow managed to hold in place, he might be able to use that stick and the grip of his right boot to push and pull himself up a bit and then there might be a bit more purchase –

There was a sound and Finbar felt himself going down. He had several disconnected thoughts, chief of which was that this was it, and then he found himself not going down any more, but clinging with mad intensity to a muddy bit of near-vertical slope and something at his feet like fucking bricks or something. Christ, he blasphemed loudly. He looked up and saw a stick fly over the side and over his head and down past him out of view. He'd gone down another good two feet or so; it was hard to tell as the rim of the pit was no longer recognisable to him, just further away.

'All right?' he said, anxiously. 'All right up there?'

'I think you'll find we're just fine, Finbar,' came Miss Donaghy's shaking voice. 'It's how you are that we're worried about.'

'I wouldn't say I'm entirely fine,' said Elizabeth. 'Ruth, *do* hold on.'

Finbar had a look at the potential climb in front of him. Two feet or so, to get back to where he'd started. He dared himself to look down. He looked down. It was really not clear but it looked like his two feet, one good one bad, were on a small ledge less than the width of a normal brick, and it didna extend either side of him more than half a foot. So there was naught here. They were going to haveta get the ropes with the clickity clips like he thought and by that point he'd have slid miserably down into the very bottom of this fucking mile-deep fucker.

'Aye. I think if I just houl on here for a bit, and as long as the school doesnae slide on top of me then I'll be all right. Some kind of wall someone built down here. It's like a shaft. Aye its a fuckin' shaft all right. And we're the ones as been shafted by it. Why'd they build a fuckin school on a fuckin shaft like this?'

'Finbar, language. There is a child here,' said Miss Donaghy.

'I think, Daphne, this may be the appropriate time for such language,' said Elizabeth.

Finbar wanted to shout loud obscenities everywhere but he bit his tongue. He glanced down again, like you can't help looking at some horrible injury or accident, just to see how bad it is. It looked worse, looked like he only had a sliver of a ledge to stand on. He needed to get the buck back up on landward. Right. Maybe even if they reached him down a thing of metal he could use it as a kind of pike to pike his way back up, mountainae climber-like. But what was he thinking? That they'd just have big lumps of sticks of metal like lyin around? He was picturing the type in the reinforced concrete but sure that's not even how the school was made except the foundations probably was, but then that'd be all covered in concrete like. He shook his head gingerly, not wishing to upset himself into the pit by doing so but he did need to do something to shake off his stupid thoughts.

'I've ninnae idea at all how to get out of here. What's up on your side?'

'We're casting about now for ideas, Finbar. How far down are you?' Miss Donaghy.

'Two foot.'

'Right. What I wouldn't give for a stretch of rope. Ok. Assuming that the whole place is going to slide down pretty soon let's just get going. Here's a beam of wood. It's long. From the roof. I'm going to slide it down and hope it hits the other side and doesn't whack you on the head. Watch your head.'

Finbar pressed himself that extra millimetre deeper into the wall of the shaft he was already as pressed into as he could be, and the big beam of wood came clattering beside him and there was a fuckload of noise and there didn't seem to be any beam lodged anywhere after it'd fallen down the tunnel but he wasn't keen to have a good look so just said 'Diddnae work to fuck. Try again.'

'We're, uh, looking for something appropriate.'

He saw Daphne Donaghy's anxious face appear at the lip of the ravine.

'Get to fuck woman!' he cried, expecting her to fall to her doom down the slippy incline right away if she dinnae step the fuck back.

'Finbar, the beam did seem to lodge a bit. I don't know how well. About three feet to your right.'

He turned his head. Looked like the girder truss he'd been sawing was now stuck at about 45° like a kind of ladder out of here. He tried craning his neck further round to see where it was connected on the other side. But couldnae. Could they see it?

'Get the fuck back from that ledge woman or you'll coup yourself and me in and before you go can you tell me is that truss stuck deep like into the other side? Cause I'm gonna havea jump it in one go cause I cannae walk over like, there's no ledge nor nuthin to stand on down here, not a fuckin causeway.'

'I can't tell, Finbar,' said Daphne, retreating from view. 'We could try ... we're looking for a plank that maybe we could lower down.'

Finbar had a vision of the three of them including the wain standing at the edge and holding a plank that they expected him to take hold of and them trying to pull him up and him being a lump them immediately falling head over down past him into the pit and him with them.

'No fear,' he shouted up, and screwed up his eyes and teeth and muscle and shut his eyes and tried to imagine an arc through space that would have him reaching gracefully around a secure girder truss ready then to pull himself up to safety. He tested his weight on his good foot. He opened his eyes again, seeing if the route he'd imagined was feasible. If he reached out his arm he could almost touch it, but that'd be no good. Needed to jump it. Needed to jump out a bit from the wall. Maybe that blackboard was still down there. He almost made an effort to jump and it reminded him of bein atop a diving board up on the high one and tryin a jump head first and not having the balls to. No. It just wasnae goina work. He was never able to jump the high jump head first off the diving board and he was never goina be able to set foot on that slithery board let alone take a leaping leap at it just to fall to his death like some diving eejit. So he'd just cling here. He'd cling here until they came with the winches and if he slipped and fell before then then that'd just be the way of it. Heart racing he clung there.

'Finbar?' came a voice – Daphne's.

'Wha?' said Finbar angrily. He wasnae angry at her it was the devil of havin about to fall in this limitless muck to die that was makin him chop his word like that.

'Finbar, we've found a way to stay secure up here. Have my feet wedged in against concrete and Liz and Ruth have me round the waist. I'm lowering one of the long curtains down to you.'

A bit of fabric hit him on the head.

'Aye fuck,' muttered Finbar under his breath. But he nervously tied the end of it round his wrist. Good solid material this. Aye maybe Daphne had a notion and he could climb up. Maybe he could climb up this. But it was the same old thing as the deep diving off a stupid pool. He'd not the cursed legs for it. *Fuckin stop you with saying you havnae the legs for it!* he told himself. Aye that was it, now the anger was turning in, and makin him ashamed of himself for not shimmying up it like mountanae goat. Right. Time to do it and not even think about it and just do it and start climbing the fuck up out of the pit up that curtainae material and away the fuck out so he put a hand up and shimmied a bit, and a bit more, and there wasn't that far te go really actually so he shimmied more but the ground all over was the same sodden slip because of the water spread all over the fuckin place and here came

Daphne and Ruth and Elizabeth Duffy to give him a hand out and he telling them 'No, get the fuck away from the edge of the bloody thing ye's'll all slip in cause it's a bloody soup!' And they backed off he was relieved as fuck to see, evidently terrified by the terror in his own voice and believing him. So he hoisted himself up and up, and then onto this wee plank of wood that was jutting out and thought it was like a lever and the further up he was the more like the thing would lift up at the other end and lose its traction and then up round and he'd be on a fuckin seesaw but it didnt happen it stayed in a place. So, down off the fucking thing into the mud but he could hold on to the curtainae stuff and pull himself along it and he rolled over on to his side once he was up a bit and looked upside down at the three of them standing there somewhere in the middle amid all the debris and wood and smashed up tables and all. He pointed unable to speak at the P4 classroom door and then got himself up off his back and on his one good foot and by now Daphne could come over and give him a hand and they hobbled to the door and Ruth and her Ma went through then the pair of them. He heard some awful bang of something falling down the pit but didnae even want to know it could go to fuck he turned his back on it and never decided to look at it again. Through into the P4/P3 storeroom then into the P4 room and then havin to crawl through that window with his leg bucked the four of them outside. Childer still going up. Get the buck up quicker and quicker he voiced but didn't say feeling something going out of him and it was the fear, even though it could all still go right down there was openness here and a calm and he felt that now though they had to move, it was ok, they'd get out and up the ladder; and so it was, waiting, for then it was Ruth and then they bullied him up being couped as he was needing to go before them, then the final pair it was Miss Donaghy and Miss McTaggart coming up, the pair of them, near fucking retirement or about a century past it in the case of thon one. Everyone panting near the top, lyin on the ground, kids huggin and shit, and cryin. He lay on his back looking at the wispy clouds, feeling he could have a fucking rollie right now but didnae have a thing. A crash from below as some other wall fell. Someone's reasonable voice saying everyone should get away from the lip of the crater as far as possible line up over there and they'd already done a roll call everyone was accounted for time to go home get some soup lie up in bed and watch TV and forget all about it. Someone dragged Finbar across the soil and propped him up against a fence and stuck a cigarette in his mouth and he puffed happily, chatted to the firemen who were on the scene looking like they'd never seen a fucking thing like it, and the ambulance men after having a prod at his foot, and wrapping some kids up in tinfoil like roasties.

'Aye the fuck,' he said, breathing out the smoke from the third ciggie he'd scobed from someone.

```
INT. MOBILE CLASSROOM - DAY

          DIRECTOR
     So that was it. The whole
     school then collapsed in
     on itself, the pit
     flooded with water, and
     that's what we can see if
     we fly a drone over the
     site. A lake where once
     there wasn't.

          DAPHNE DONAGHY
```

>   In a nutshell. What are
>   you going to do now,
>   stick the rolling credits
>   on?
>
>   DIRECTOR
>   Hardly. We've only begun
>   to scratch the surface of
>   this disaster. There's
>   all the subsequent trauma
>   to explore. How the kids
>   have reacted. My main
>   regret is we haven't got
>   footage.   I'll
>   dramatically recreate it
>   with some arts council
>   funding. Or a grant from
>   one of the terrestrial
>   stations. Now I've got
>   this, they'll be all over
>   it. I sent off my first
>   application yesterday.

THE HISTORY OF THE PERLOUGH SALT MINE

Records are scant and few. Since Sir Houldsworth-Farrington abandoned the Perlough Estate in 1877 for the east coast of the United States presumably he had no further interest in the land. Either all the viable salt was removed or it was simply uneconomic to continue. There were several disadvantages to the site, the chief being its remoteness from efficient forms of transport like rail or sea. On cost terms it could not compete even with the Downshire mines, better served on both counts. Of course, as long as demand was high this simply meant lower profit margins. But by 1877 something else had changed and, it is believed, the shaft was boarded over and the site abandoned.

For a period in the 1890s the shaft apparently was uncovered again, for there are reports of local children finding enjoyment by rolling boulders down it and waiting for the enormous crashes that ensued.

Later the cavern was flooded in order to facilitate downstream extraction of brine, though when this happened is not known for certain. Importantly, this most likely created further structural weaknesses contributing to the much later collapse of the lower half of Perlough Primary School.

How it came to pass that the entire history of the site faded from memory is not known but by 1909 when building commenced on Perlough Primary School no-one living voiced any concerns. By the time the lower wing was built in the latter decades of the 20th century no trace of the shaft was discernible. This is a remarkable fact given that one wall of the P3 classroom lay less than a metre from the edge of a 600 foot pit. The most likely explanation is that topsoil had been spread to a depth of several metres over the site rendering evidence of a shaft or of mineworks less obvious to those erecting the new wing of the primary school. As to why topsoil was spread out this way we have no clear knowledge. It may have simply been to level the heap of extracted rock created in the digging of the principal shaft.

As to the precipitating event causing the dramatic collapse of the lower wing of Perlough Primary, here only our imagination can fill in the details. Whether deliberately flooded or not, water inevitably reached the caverns dug deep underground and the salt pillars were eroded. It is common in historical salt mines to have wide pillars supporting the upper roof. Other salt mines in the area from the time had two levels, this prehistoric salt bed having apparently been formed twice with a layer of dense impermeable rock several metres thick between the two. Any one of the many pillars supporting either cavern may have finally been unable to support the load and fallen, bringing the roof with it. Likely this was a pillar near the original shaft since, as we know, this was the site of most notable land settlement and which swallowed most of the P3 classroom.

All that can be seen now of the site is a calm, languid pool. This can only be seen by drone or some other aerial method; the site is restricted from access to a distance of one hundred metres every direction from the central shaft. Exploratory drilling, performed immediately after the collapse, confirmed there were no other pits in the Perlough area. Careful examination of historical maps seems to confirm this. As to why this historical documentation was not consulted in the original construction of the school or the lower wing we have no answers. There is no obvious talk of legal liability or compensation payments. School boards, local politicians, parents, teachers and children alike seem happy in their conspiracy to move on and forget it. To let it dissolve in memory, erode like an unseen pillar of salt; to let water fill up the terrible shear visible in the surface, soften those lines, and pretend that nothing lies beneath we need be afraid of.

DOWN THE MINE (FINAL PART)

Thomas lay on his back wondering where he was. He lay there for a few more minutes. Everything ached. All was black and silent. Something had happened. But he wasn't sure what. His fingers felt funny.

He tried to sit up.

'Sweet Jesus,' he said, but he couldn't hear his own voice.

For a while, he sat there, confused. He had a sense that something terrible had happened. At the same time he felt a sense of relief which, having no reason for itself, was even more confusing. He got onto his hands and knees. He felt out with his hands in a circle, trying to get a sense of where he was and what was going on.

He was in the mine because the ground was coarse and (licking his fingers) salty. He touched something that felt like material. Under the material something like a person. For a moment he kept his hand there. Dust, warm, down the mine. No hearing, someone lying on the ground. He couldn't reach a conclusion. He sat up. He patted his pockets, trying to remember where he kept his matches. He took out the box and struck a match. It flared. He watched it burn. He struck another match, watched it, dropped it.

He tried to shout. No sound, although it felt like he was shouting. He wondered what his shout sounded like. No-one above would hear him.

The idea suddenly occurred to him that he might be trapped. A rising sense of panic. He wanted to run. Run where? You might not be trapped, Thomas. Feel about. Get a sense of where. Who's this I'm beside?

He had a memory of coming down the shaft and stepping out. He couldn't remember who had followed. Elbert. He felt along the body up to the face. It didn't feel right. Moustache, not Elbert. Something had happened. The good thing was Thomas wasn't dead. But this other man, he would have to drag him out and back up the shaft. Room for two. It'd be all right. But he'd need to see a way. He'd need a light. He'd need burn some thing, on a stick or what. There'd be sticks here. There'd be bleedin' dynamite too; better watch for that. Needed a stick. Feeling around for one. Feel, feel, feel, like one of those scuttling things at the sea. Found it. What was it? Bit of a stick with the end off. Just a stick. Fine. Take off my shirt here, wrap that round. Should burn, shouldn't it? Bleeding heart, what about the dynamite? Don't light anything. Feel about. Or go the hell away somewhere … No, this here, be the same anywhere. Right, light it. Come on my shaking hands. Awkwardly resting the makeshift torch between his legs cupping the flame of a lit match and attempting to light the tightly wrapped shirt. It caught on a third attempt. Cautiously he lifted the torch. It revealed the person casting an eery shadow over the glistening ground. Who was it? It was Henry, not looking right, not looking the way a man should. Aye, it was Henry McKnicken all right. Thomas stared, the shadows dancing around the man. That was his chest moving. Or was it the dancing shadows? Thomas turned away. He held the torch high, trying to get a sense of his environment. Load wires. Stones on the ground. Mess. Rough surface. Be hell trying to drag a man over. How would he get anywhere, with Henry on his arm and a torch held in the other?

    He gathered a pile of stones so he had enough to jimmy the torch into it. Yonder seemed the route. He took a swift stroll into the darkness. Got dark fast. Had a sense from the air. Like a little note you could barely feel of freshness. Meant something was getting through or it was his own madness. He went back and cursed McKnicken for being a heavy lump. He dragged him towards that little whisper of air. Back again for the torch. It was near out. What, take off his trousers and all? Henry … he didn't want to start. Trousers. They'd laugh at him but better to be laughin up there with no trousers than stuck down here with them on. Trousers off. Wrapped round. Take it over and make a wee heap of stones jimmy it in. Right ye lug me and you again. If you're dead I'll kill you. Wake up and give us a hand. That whisper. Should have scouted. Go get the torch. Don't trip on that, what the hell it is. Was Henry the only?

Do I need to look over? Ah, I don't know. One at a time. Bring him up first then ask. Someone else can go down. Ouch, I can feel it. Musta done something me arm because Henry wouldn't hurt like this if I wasn't hurt he's lighter than a sackful of rock. But more difficult not the right shape. Come on come on. Is that what's it? Looks like something I can see which means something that is lit. Or am I seeing the fire in my eyes? It's the right way, its where that sliver of air is coming from. Aye, there's a pillar there, big thick brute the one they wanted special beside the shaft in case it fell they didna want to have to dig another. Doesn't matter if the other bits fall, can just dig it out and with me in it. Back over. Should've kept me trousers on. Should've taken Henry's he can afford another pair. Heavy bastard. Why isnae my arm working? Come on. Dragging half the mine with you. Lift your feet man. Another hundred yards is it can't be maybe ten. There's the light that's light we're near the entrance to the tunnel. That's the tube. Why's it on its side? Get back up ye bastard thing. Just what I need heaviest bloody thing in the world. At least the cord. Up. How are we going to swing back and forth like a bleedin pendulum there and not smash every wall we come to? Maybe I should just put him in and pull the cord but he can't sit up so it'll be all over. Up, my hands round him like this and if I pull you over me again maybe I twist one way if it looks like we're goin the other. Christ forgive me. Hand up and pull that bell, pull, pull, pay attention up there you sods and get me quickly up stop sipping you tea and get us out.

Stephen McSonder and wee Rick wondered if Thomas had got on a drunk the thing was swingin' so much.

'Christ, he'll bang a hole in the side of the shaft if he keeps goin' like that. Slow the thing down til it stops there! Aye, let him dangle. We've had nobody whack in the wall yet but he's a mind down there to be the first. Must be Henry. He's no notion of getting in or out.'

'What's he comin up for anyway?' asked Rick, panting with the exertion. At a signal from the other man he resumed turning the wooden handle. The gears cranked.

'The hell I know. Probably he forgot his lunch up here. I'd known I would of ate it.'

The tube came slowly up. When it reached the rim of the shaft Stephen McSonder put the brake on the line to reached over and grab it. It was bloody heavy that tin can and sooner or later someone'd coup trying to tack it up. The trick was to get hold of the handle when it was swinging and bring it up and over in one go. Hook it up. Draw it round.

It took some work but they did it and waited for Henry to come out. But they heard Thomas shouting whether they could hear him and if they could get him and Henry out he had no hands to open up.

Stephen glanced at Rick. They opened the door and Thomas fell out almost backwards holding on to Henry. Or they thought it was Henry but he didn't look right; not right at all. In fact, he looked dead.

Thomas felt morning light on his face. Felt as if he had not ever slept. A deep emptiness was in him, deep as the shaft.

He had to get up. He had to get up today or it was the end. Twice now he'd been to the works and twice now looked down that deep pit and not been able to descend. Why had he lived? Sure he'd lived, that's what they said. They said you was the one that lived and the court exonerated you. Since you couldn't remember and there were no witnesses there was no case.

Thomas couldn't remember. It had been dark and Henry lying on the ground and him taking Henry out and then he was up. No-one knew the how or why. They said it looked like Henry'd been standing too near the face when a stone hit him. Who'd done the blowing? Henry? No-one knew. All they knew was the dynamite and where to stand and how to fire it. Thomas knew and Henry knew. Nothing should have happened but the man was dead. It seemed to go deeper than the salt mines. It seemed to go deeper than anything could go but he'd have to get up. There was a wain on the way. A life to replace a life. He couldn't go back. He'd have to go back though. But he couldn't go back. But he'd have to go back though.


```
EXT. WATER - DUSK

Shot of shimmering water.
Shot of sky.
Shot of sky seen from within water.

                        FADE OUT.



                  THE END
```

THANK YOU!

Thank you for reading this book. I'd love to hear what you think, so if you find time to leave a review on Amazon I'd be very grateful. Email me the URL to your review and I'll send you a review copy of one of my other books: *Shorter Than The Day* or *Aliens Versus Football*. Email me which book you'd like to review and I'll send it to you for free. My email address is erwanatcheson@gmail.com

Subscribe to my mailing list and monthly newsletter at:

subscribepage.io/erwan